1976

University of St. Francis

S0-BEQ-147

3 0301 00031545 3

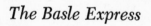

The Basle Express

British Intelligence agent Tommy Hambledon had the mistaken notion when he arrived at Innsbruck that he had left behind all connections with Herr Bastien, who had been shot in the railway compartment they shared on the Anglo-Swiss Express. But when he was commanded by a belligerent Austrian taxi driver to disrobe, and then forced at gunpoint to hike barefoot over the Alps, Hambledon ruefully decided that his vacation was over.

With the help of a horse-faced English tourist—and over the opposition of some escaped lunatics, an enormously stout gentleman with a feather in his hat, a village idiot, and a Communist named Medeski—Tommy Hambledon unravels this gripping and intrigue-ridden international mystery.

Scene: Central Europe.
This novel has not appeared in any form prior to book publication.

MANNING COLES

The Basle Express

DOUBLEDAY & COMPANY, INC.

GARDEN CITY, NEW YORK

LIBRARY
College of St. Francis
JOLIET, ILL.

All of the characters in this book are fictitious and any resemblance to actual persons, living or dead, is purely coincidental.

LC # 56-5438

Copyright © 1956
By Doubleday & Company, Inc.
All Rights Reserved
Printed in the United States of America

823
C696L

To Charles L. Fackler
of York, Pennsylvania

Old roads winding, as old roads will.
J. G. WHITTIER

74976

CONTENTS

CAST

Thomas Elphinstone Hambledon, *of British Intelligence.*

Edouard Gilles Bastien, *a journalist.*

Pierre, *his murderer.*

Virolet, *Detective-Inspector of Police at Metz.*

Cournand, *Superintendent of Police at Basle.*

Eugene ⎫
Erich ⎬ Crooks.
Paulus Caron ⎭

Alexis Medeski *of the U.S.S.R. Diplomatic Service.*

Lucius Lombard, *a traveller in mouth organs.*

A. G. Eisenschmidt, *antique dealer in Innsbruck.*

Gustav Norz, *owner of the antique shop.*

Horaz, *an odd-job man.*

Agatha Wiggins, *a travelling Englishwoman.*

Grissemann *and* Geisler, *perfectly harmless.*

The Herren Bauer & Schollhorn, *psychiatrists.*

Police, innkeepers, waiters, hotel guests, gangsters, etc.

The Basle Express

CHAPTER I

A Man Named Pierre

The Anglo-Swiss Express, loaded as its name suggests with the travelling English, leaves Calais at twenty minutes to seven in the evening and rumbles through the night, with only five stops on the way, to reach Basle at six in the morning. One dines, one sleeps, one wakes in the morning and there is Switzerland. At least, that is the general idea, and most people carry it out more or less.

Thomas Elphinstone Hambledon intended to do so. He had dined and found somebody to talk to over his coffee, *fine,* and cigarette. The time was getting on; there would be an early rise in the morning and he was getting sleepy. He decided to return to the sleeper which he shared with another man about whom he knew nothing except that he was an elderly man who wrote for the Press, intended to retire shortly and thereafter pursue a recently acquired enthusiasm for making model ships.

When Hambledon reached his sleeper he found his companion for the night already in pyjamas and bed, sitting up smoking cigarettes and browsing happily through the pages of a book which he had already recommended to Hambledon's attention, *How to Make Old-Time Ship Models* by one E. W. Hobbs.

"Still studying your bible?" asked Hambledon pleasantly.

The man looked up with a smile. He had dark wiry hair going

silver at the temples and thin on the crown, his fingers were stained with nicotine, and his face was deeply lined and wore a habitually sardonic expression. He spoke fluent English but with a perceptible foreign accent.

"That is so. I find it pleasant to study it and to say to myself, some day I will build that, and that."

"Tell me," said Hambledon, proceeding with his undressing, "what does one do with ship models when they are finished?"

"The usual procedure is to set them upon the tops of bookcases where they either become wreathed in dust and cobwebs or else receive daily damage from daily cleaning. Or else they are put in glass cases."

"Or given to nephews."

"I have no nephews. No. I do not purpose to follow any of these courses. I propose that my ships shall sail. Sir, you look surprised, but why should they not if properly ballasted? Their prototypes did."

"Certainly," said Hambledon amiably, "indeed they did. Drake went round the world in the *Golden Hind,* though I don't know that I should have cared to accompany him."

"There is an illustration here," said the stranger, "of a model of the *Golden Hind,* look."

"She looks a bit top-heavy," said Hambledon. He began to turn over the pages of the book, but its owner took it from him.

"Excuse me, there are some folded plans interleaved; if they fall out and become unfolded it is a nuisance. Yes, she looks top-heavy but with proper ballasting—sir, what could be more delightful than to see with one's own eyes these famous vessels ploughing the water again as they did four hundred years ago?"

Hambledon paused in the act of getting into his bunk.

"You know, I do see your point there. Like looking back at history through the wrong end of a telescope. Yes, I should like to see that myself." He climbed into bed and switched out his reading lamp.

"I hope you sleep well," said the stranger. "Sir, with simple pride I assure you that I do not snore."

"I have never been accused of that either," laughed Hambledon, "though I understand that one cannot tell with regard to one's self."

"You are not married then? Nor I. It is better so," said the other man, putting *How to Make Old-Time Ship Models* on the little flap table under the window and switching out his light. "One can change one's housekeeper."

The compartment was lighted only by a small blue lamp in the roof and blinds were drawn over the windows at both ends. The train stopped at Mézières and, after a long pause, moved on again. Hambledon grew drowsy, listening to the various train noises which merged more and more remotely into a mere background of sound as he fell asleep.

He woke suddenly from a dream in which some man was trying to tell him something terribly urgent but was speaking so quietly that his voice was inaudible. The dream vanished but the voice went on, addressing not Hambledon but the occupant of the other bunk; the language used was French.

"Keep your voice down," it said; "there is no need to awaken that other. You will hand over those papers at once and without fuss, Monsieur Bastien."

"My good idiot," said Bastien yawning audibly, "I have no idea what you are talking about. There is the London *Times* on the rack, also today's *Temps* and the latest *New Yorker* if you want something to read."

The newcomer said, "Stop this fooling at once. Those papers you got by a trick at Basle last night. Give them to me."

"But——"

"Look. This is a gun. Do you want to die?"

"Not particularly," drawled Bastien.

"Then you'd better hand over. Where are they? Where——"

"In my despatch case——"

"Let me get up."

"Certainly not. What for?"

"Because I'm lying on it, fool. Do you suppose I'd leave it about where any cheap train thief could sneak it?"

The intruder, who had been bending over Bastien, moved back. Hambledon, through half-closed eyes, could see him plainly, gun and all, so bright did the dim blue light appear to eyes accustomed to it. Hambledon was the victim of extreme indecision; he had no weapon himself, and few postures are more impeding to action than being under bedclothes well tucked in. Besides, it might be true that Bastien had stolen whatever it was the other man wanted; if Bastien were prepared to hand it back presumably the intruder would depart satisfied and all would be well.

Bastien swung his legs out of bed and stood up; the train rocked and bumped over points and both men staggered.

"Be quick," said the intruder, "be quick. This is Metz and I get off here."

Bastien began to feel among the bedclothes and under the mattress; it was plain that he was putting off time, and the train began to slow down.

"Hurry! Name of ten thousand devils—I will kill you in ten seconds from now——"

"I forgot," said Bastien calmly, "it is on the rack, after all." He pointed at the luggage rack above his bunk and the man looked up towards it and the light. There was a despatch case on the rack.

"I thought I knew your voice," said Bastien, "Pierre——"

"Unlucky for you," snarled Pierre, and shot him through the head. Before Bastien's body had slid to the floor Pierre had snatched the despatch case from the rack, flung the door open, and was in the corridor before Hambledon was out of bed. There was a startled exclamation outside, an angry snarl and a cry of pain. Hambledon shot out into the corridor just in time to provide the staggering *conducteur* with someone to cling to. The train slowed abruptly and platform lights slid past the windows. Pierre had gone.

"Stop that man——" began Hambledon.

"My head—one has struck me on the head——"

The passing lights became slower and slower yet; from the end of the corridor there came a gust of cold air as somebody opened a door.

"He'll get away," said Hambledon, vainly trying to disconnect himself from the *conducteur* whose knees were giving way. A door slammed at the end of the next coach and Hambledon saw a figure he recognized running to a stop beside the still moving train. The next moment Pierre turned away and disappeared.

"Well, I'm not going to chase him in pyjamas and bare feet," said Hambledon irritably. "Hold up, man. Pull yourself together; there's been murder done—I think."

"Murder?" said the man dazedly. "Oh, no. I am hurt but I am not dead. Indeed, not."

"I rejoice," said Hambledon. " Nevertheless a gentleman has been shot in my compartment. Should we not go and see whether he lives or not?"

The *conducteur* removed his arms from round Hambledon's neck, drew himself up and said, "Lead on, monsieur," in a solemn leaden voice. "Which compartment?"

Bastien was not quite dead when they picked him up and laid him on the bed. The *conducteur* bent over him.

"Monsieur, can you speak? Monsieur, who did this?"

Bastien's eyes opened for a moment, and it is possible that he saw Hambledon.

"Albert," he murmured, "Albert." He died at once.

"Albert," repeated the *conducteur*. "Might that perhaps be your name, monsieur?"

"Certainly not," said Hambledon coldly.

"Then it is that of his assassin."

Hambledon opened his mouth, shut it again and finally said, "You must summon the police. At once. This train must be held here."

"Impossible——"

"Go," said Hambledon, pushing him out into the corridor, "go and call the police. Instantly." He slid the doors together behind the *conducteur* and began hastily to dress.

The doors slid open and one of the railway police came in. His eyes widened as he saw Bastien's body on the left-hand bunk. Hambledon asked if there were any objection to his staying in the compartment for as long as it would take him to dress himself. "Pyjamas," he said affably, "and bare feet are not suitable wear for these tragic occasions. They lower the morale."

"Undoubtedly, monsieur. I am not, myself, in charge of this case. I am merely here until the civil police arrive, but I cannot see any objection to monsieur dressing himself. Even in the highly inconceivable event of the civil police arresting monsieur, he would still be allowed to dress before being taken to the police station."

"Eh? I didn't shoot this poor man."

"I did not say that monsieur did. On the contrary, I said that the idea was inconceivable."

"Then why conceive it?"

"Precisely, monsieur," said the policeman, and twirled his moustache. The door slid open again and a gendarme beckoned the first man out.

"I'll take over now," said the gendarme. "You run along and count parcels. Good evening, monsieur. This is a nasty business. Our head office is sending down dectectives and so on, and they said would you be so good as to stay here till they come."

"Certainly," said Hambledon, knotting his tie and putting on his waistcoat.

"All these clothes on the floor," said the gendarme in an enquiring voice.

"They are his, not mine. Mine were still hanging up as I left them."

"Then we'd best not touch them. These dectectives, they become as tigers if the smallest alteration is made."

"Very true," said Hambledon, putting his coat on and sitting down on his bunk. "Do you think your superiors would mind if I had a cigarette? Good. Will you join me?"

"I thank monsieur, not at the moment." He glanced over his shoulder. "Here is Monsieur Virolet." He retired modestly into the corridor and came to attention.

A thin dark man with a drooping black moustache came to stand in the doorway and survey the scene. He nodded to Hambledon—"Just a moment, monsieur"—leaned against the doorpost, took a crumpled packet of Gaulois Bleu cigarettes from his pocket, and absent-mindedly put one in his mouth. Instantly a hand holding a petrol lighter came round the detective's shoulder, applied a flame to his cigarette, and vanished again. Virolet took not the slightest notice of this and slowly but thoroughly let his eyes travel all over the compartment. When he had finished his survey he turned to Hambledon and introduced himself.

"My name is Virolet," he said, and added his rank which was equivalent to Detective Inspector. Hambledon said that the meeting would have been a pleasure if the circumstances had been less fortunate, and gave Virolet one of his official cards.

"Monsieur Hambledon of British Intelligence? But this is a pleasure. I have heard of you from an old friend, Letord of the Sûreté, do you remember? A case about some forged currency in Brussels, yes. We will talk about him later. In the meantime this is my miserable downtrodden assistant, Detective Sergeant Arnoux. He does all the work while I stand about and find fault."

Virolet moved out of the doorway to diclose the presence of Arnoux who was, Hambledon thought, quite the smallest police-man he had ever seen. The French do not seem to have any size qualifications for entry into their police forces; so long as a man is intelligent and fit and of a certain educational standard he may serve. Perhaps the smaller ones take courses in jujitsu to level things up. Arnoux may have been an inch over five feet but no more. He had a round cheerful face and a compact figure with small hands and feet. He must have been stronger than he looked, for he was carrying the "murder bag," a large leather bag of the Gladstone type from which he drew a big old-fashioned wooden camera. The unusually large pockets in his raincoat were dragged down by the weight of dark slides.

"One from the doorway, Arnoux, and then some close-ups," said Virolet, turning on every available light.

"I'll come out in the corridor," said Hambledon. "I am in your way."

"Impossible, monsieur," said Arnoux politely, but stood back to let him pass. The sergeant was plainly used to handling his big camera, for he swung it up without effort and took a couple of exposures from the doorway; he was so quick at handling his dark slides that the process was but little slower than wind-ing on a film. He advanced into the compartment to take close-up shots of the unfortunate Bastien; the double-extension bellows was racked out till it looked like the trunk of an inquisitive elephant.

"He'll never hold that thing steady," said Hambledon.

"Oh yes he will," said Virolet. "He generally does. Who is the victim, did you know him?"

"Never met him till tonight," answered Hambledon. "He told me that he wrote for the Press and his assailant called him Monsieur Bastien."

"I seem to have heard that name. Those are his clothes on the floor, are they? One of the clothes on the floor, Arnoux. I suppose he didn't have the kindness to name his assailant, did he?"

"He said: 'I thought I knew your voice, Pierre—' and then Pierre shot him."

"It would be Pierre," said the detective in a resigned voice. "It is the name of twenty-five per cent of the male population of France. It is even my own. Why could not his parents have christened him Heliogabalus or Cincinnatus? Finished, Arnoux? Come out of the way while I look at these clothes."

Arnoux wriggled round his superior officer into the corridor and handed the dark slides he had used out of the window to someone outside who had apparently been waiting there for that purpose, for he set off at a run. Hambledon, who did not wish to appear inquisitive, left Virolet examining the clothes and leaned out of the window. One would think that most of the police force of Metz were there upon the platform discouraging any who wished to draw near that coach; there were policemen at the doors and stationed in the corridor while, even as Hambledon looked out, there approached a small group of sturdy men carrying a stretcher. Another man carrying a small black bag hurried through the police cordon and proved to be what he looked, a doctor. Hambledon felt a touch on his arm and looked round.

"Those clothes had been thoroughly searched," said Virolet, "even to slitting the seams."

"That would be before I woke," said Hambledon. "It was the sound of talking which roused me though they were almost whispering."

"We will tell the *chef de train* to find us an empty compartment, and you shall tell me what you know. Arnoux——" But the little man had already darted away. "The motive was not robbery," went on Virolet, "here is his wallet with plenty of money in it. Here is his passport, too, he was Edouard Gilles Bastien with an address in Basle; profession, Press Correspondent. He left Basle last night, here is the exit stamp."

"Pierre said that Bastien was in Basle last night," said Hambledon. "He said that Bastien had got some papers by a trick and Pierre wanted them back. He said he would shoot Bastien if he didn't hand them over, and Bastien said they were in his despatch case on the rack. Pierre looked up, the light from that blue night lamp fell on his face, and Bastien recognized him and was rash enough to say so."

"And that is why he was shot, no doubt, since he was giving up the papers. Here come the rest of my gang, though I don't suppose it will be the slightest use fingerprinting in here." Hambledon prepared to withdraw and Virolet said, "I wonder if the *chef de train* has a spare—there he is. Arnoux——"

"If Monsieur Hambledon would have the goodness to come this way, there is an empty compartment; it is a day coach, but——"

"That doesn't matter," said Hambledon. "My things——There is only a rucksack, a coat, and some magazines."

"I will send a man along with them in a moment and come myself as soon as I can," said Virolet. "Here, doctor."

Hambledon effaced himself but not before he had heard a wail coming in through the open corridor window.

"Monsieur Virolet! Cannot the train go on? I am the station-master. I implore you to allow——"

Virolet said something inaudible, and the stationmaster's high voice rose again.

"But one does not hold the Anglo-Swiss Express! One——"

Hambledon was conducted to a vacant compartment in the next coach. A suitcase, an overcoat, and two brown paper parcels were being removed by a porter.

"Someone has been turned out to make room for us?"

"Certainly, monsieur," said the *chef de train.*

"He—or she—did not object?"

"Monsieur, we said that it was an anxious parent with a sick and weeping child; would the passenger permit that they share his compartment which was otherwise empty. Monsieur, he begged to be allowed to resign the entire compartment to the prior claims of maternal solicitude."

"Magnificent," said Hambledon.

"Not at all," said the *chef de train* modestly. "All part of the service, monsieur."

He went away; a moment later the doors reopened to admit a policeman with Hambledon's rucksack, overcoat, and roll of magazines. The man put the things down, asked if that were all or was there anything more, and went away reassured. Hamble-don got up to hang his coat upon a hook and a book slipped to the floor from under it—*How to Make Old-Time Ship Models.*

"Poor old chap," said Tommy, and tossed the book on the opposite seat.

CHAPTER II

Newspaper Correspondent

Eventually the train started again, no doubt to the delight of the stationmaster of Metz who could see his whole local system being disorganized, and a few minutes later Virolet came in accompanied by Arnoux. Virolet said that somebody was bringing some probably horribly inferior coffee if monsieur would join them in a cup, and they sat down heavily.

"Were you in bed," asked Hambledon sympathetically, "when this call came?"

"Oh no. We were merely hoping to go shortly. We only had four hours in bed the night before, eh, Arnoux?"

"Three hours and forty minutes, me," said Arnoux cheerfully. "The Inspector lives ten minutes nearer the station than I do."

"Another murder?"

"Oh, no. An absconding bank manager, much more urgent. There are so many lives in this world, are there not, monsieur? But money, no. Very short supply."

A man came to the door with a tray of three thick cups of coffee and handed it around. Virolet took one and looked at it dubiously.

"This the best you can do?"

"All I can do, monsieur," said the man with emphasis. "Breakfast, at Basle, monsieur."

"Go away," said Virolet and the door closed behind the man. "This," went on the Inspector, "is, no doubt, one degree better than a nice glass of cold water. This is your book, monsieur?"

"No," said Hambledon, "it was Bastien's actually. It came along here with my things. I was going to give it to you."

The Inspector dipped into it, looking at the photographs while he drank his coffee; he closed the book and gave it to Hambledon.

"Accept a memento of a disturbed night, monsieur. When I have time for that kind of thing I shall be a nice new angel in Paradise. Well now, if you will be so good as to tell me everything that happened?"

Hambledon did so, including a detailed description, in the police manner, of Pierre, and Arnoux took shorthand notes.

"The Basle police may know him," said Virolet. "I shall come through to Basle on this train, have that coach put into a siding and that compartment efficiently searched. I did have a quick look a it but one never knows. Besides, if the Basle police will do it, I shall not have to fatigue myself, eh?"

"His luggage," began Hambledon.

"One suitcase. I sent a man to my office with it. No, if, as I assume, those papers were in the despatch case, I do not imagine that there is anything left for us to find. Why should there be? These papers we have nowadays! Anything from atomic bomb secrets to blackmail letters beginning 'My angel cabbage' and signed 'Thine Adorer.' Phoo! They are lost, stolen, read by those not intended to read them, sold to Foreign Powers, left in trains, taxis, cafés, *boîtes de nuit,* put in the wrong envelopes and posted. And who has to look for them?"

"Quite often," said Hambledon, "me."

"Precisely! And me. All this education," said Virolet passionately, "is a great mistake. As regards Bastien, I do not suppose that there is anything in the affair. He was a newspaper reporter, probably he had annoyed somebody. Pierre we will catch if we can—what, in your opinion, was his nationality, monsieur?"

"French. Southern France. *Marseillais,* perhaps."

The train began to slow down. Arnoux drew the blind aside and looked out of the window.

"Strasbourg?" asked Virolet.

"Yes, monsieur. Strasbourg."

Hambledon sighed suddenly and turned sideways in his corner; the night was proving rather long. The train stopped at last and a few doors slammed in the distance. He looked at his watch.

"What a time," he said, "to alight at Strasbourg. Twenty minutes past four."

"We are making up time," said Arnoux. "We were thirty-five minutes late leaving Metz."

"Who cares?" said Virolet wearily. He leaned back in his corner and closed his eyes. The compartment door slid open and the *chef de train* stood there with an envelope in his hand.

"A message for Detective Inspector Virolet."

Arnoux took the note, tore open the envelope, and presented the message to Virolet all in one movement. Virolet looked at it and said, "No reply, thank you." The *chef de train* went out and the doors slid together again.

"Pierre did not find his papers in the despatch case," said Virolet.

"How?" said Hambledon.

"I told you I sent Bastien's suitcase to my office by one of my men? Yes. He was knocked on the head on his way to the station and the suitcase stolen."

"Dead?" asked Arnoux.

"Oh, no. He has a headache, I imagine. He will have another when I see him again. It was in that little alley called the Boyau. Do you know Metz, monsieur?"

"No. Not well."

"It is a short cut to the police station," said Arnoux.

"But that is no reason why a man should walk along it with his eyes shut," said Virolet. "Especially a policeman."

"I wonder whether the papers were in the suitcase," said Hambledon idly.

"So do I. Monsieur Hambledon, why did Bastien say 'Albert' when he was dying? Can you think of any reason?"

"Who can tell what may rise in the mind of a dying man? Especially when he has been shot in the head. It is, of course, a place name, if that's any help."

"It is, yes."

The train stopped again at Mulhouse, but Hambledon was asleep and did not notice it, nor were any more messages handed in, and they reached Basle punctually at six.

74976

College of St. Francis Library
Joliet, Illinois

"Bath and breakfast," said Hambledon cheerfully, for sleep had refreshed him.

"I agree. Will you breakfast with me, monsieur? My programme is the same as yours except that I must telephone the Swiss police first."

"With pleasure, thank you. We will meet in the restaurant, then."

Basle station may be said to be the centre of the spider's web of the railway systems of Western Europe. In Paris one arrives at any one of half-a-dozen main-line stations and there will be an exhilarating taxi drive to the other; at Basle there is the one big station and it is said that unless a man is prepared to say at home all his life, sooner or later he will breakfast there. This is no hardship, for the restaurant is famous, especially for black cherry jam, and the bathrooms are almost equally in demand.

Hambledon, pink and clean, shaven and brushed, came into the restaurant, wandered from room to room looking for Virolet, and was found by Arnoux.

"I have a table in the room with the scenery down the middle, if you will follow me," said the Detective Sergeant. "The Inspector's compliments and he begs you not to wait for him. He will be with you shortly."

The scenery down the middle consists of pot plants on a low partition, but they are a pleasant sight in the early morning. Hambledon had not finished his first cup of coffee before Virolet came striding in with Arnoux at his heels.

"The police here are most friendly and helpful," said Virolet, "always. I have done business with them before. That train we came in is put onto a siding to be washed and tidied up for the run back to Calais tonight; the Swiss police are asking the stationmaster to leave that locked compartment untouched. One of them—yes, coffee, please, and rolls—a man named Cournand is coming here to meet us and we will do the coach together. Is monsieur still interested? Perhaps you would care to accompany us. Cournand is a nice fellow and only mad on one subject. The ballet. Is monsieur also a balletomane, if I have the term correctly?"

"In the matter of the ballet," said Hambledon, "I am painfully uncultured."

"And I. Tell me, how do they spin round like tops and not get giddy? That is what I ask myself. For me, if I spin round rapidly three times, the room comes with me."

"Perhaps it is practice," suggested Hambledon.

"Probably," agreed Virolet. Then, with another of his rapid changes of subject: "Monsieur is going to Innsbruck, you said, did you not?"

"I am, actually, going to Seefeld in the Tyrol. One changes at Innsbruck and there is an hour in a local train. I am due for a holiday, and some friends of mine told me the place was charming."

"I have heard so, yes. One climbs mountains, I believe. Monsieur is a mountaineer, no doubt? I see you have a rucksack. But there are plenty of trains from here to Innsbruck. Here is Cournand in person."

Cournand, a short stocky man with a slow smile and a pleasant manner, came up and was introduced.

"So you have been letting somebody get murdered in one of your dangerous trains, eh? You should take more care of your customers, Virolet. For me," he added to Hambledon, "whenever I have to travel upon the French railway systems I insure my life."

"I am not a railway official," said Virolet mildly.

"If you were I would not travel at all! Terrible people, these French. Tell me, whom have you killed off this time?"

"A man named Bastien, a newspaper correspondent. He lived in Basle according to his passport. Do you know him?"

"Know him? I should think so. He is very well known, our Herr Bastien. He has been at the game a very long time; he was not young. Sixty, perhaps? His birthdate will be on his passport. He was very wise and experienced; he knew everybody, absolutely everybody, Herr Hambledon. Not only celebrities but also waiters, taxidrivers, porters, flower sellers, café proprietors, everyone. Not only in Basle, but in Geneva, in Rome, in Bonn, in Paris, who knows? He would stroll round talking to his friends; if your Sir Anthony Eden bought himself a new hat, Bastien was the first to hear of it."

"Political stuff, eh? What paper did he write for?" asked Hambledon.

"No one paper. He was, as they say, a free lance. It was very

careless of you, Virolet my friend, to let such a man be shot—
who did it?"

"A man named Pierre; perhaps you know him too. Monsieur
Hambledon saw it done, and here is his description." The break-
fast room had emptied; there was no one to overhear them.
"Arnoux, read it out."

Arnoux did so. Cournand listened and shook his head.

"No, I cannot place him. Please let me have a copy of that
and I will ask my men. Somebody may know him if he has ever
lived here. Have you reason to think he has?"

Hambledon repeated Pierre's remark to Bastien about "those
papers you got by a trick at Basle last night" and added, "Of
course, that doesn't prove that Pierre was also in Basle that night,
or ever. He may have been told that over the telephone."

Cournand brooded, staring at the tablecloth, and then roused
himself.

"Have you all finished? Quite sure? Then let us go and examine the scene of the crime. We will get a railway official to lead
us to it; I have no ambition to end my life in small pieces under
the wheels of a locomotive. Shall we go?"

"Monsieur Hambledon," said Virolet, "where is your luggage?"

"In the left-luggage office."

Virolet nodded.

They followed a railway man for about a half mile across lines
and along tracks, a most uncomfortable walk, until they climbed
into the sleeping car of last night's Anglo-Swiss Express. The
other coaches were all being energetically swept and polished by
the cleaners, but the whole of that particular coach had been
left until they had seen it. Virolet led the way along the corridor
to the compartment which had been left locked and stopped
short at the door with a loud exclamation.

The doors were no longer locked but ajar, and the inside of
the compartment was a wreck. Bedclothes lay on the floor in a
sordid tangle, mattresses were flung awry, and the padding of
the seats had been slit and dragged out to open up the crevices
between. The four men viewed the scene in silence broken eventually by Virolet.

"The papers were not in the suitcase," he said.

Cournand turned on his heel and leaned out of the corridor

window, shouting for the foreman in charge of the cleaners who came running.

"Mein Herr?"

"This coach," said Cournand, "was ordered to be left uncleaned until we, the police, had examined it, was it not?"

"Certainly, mein Herr, and so it was. Even now we have not started on it, as you can see."

"Yes," said Cournand, "yes." Did you see the police who examined it, then?"

"I saw them, yes. When we arrived I saw some men—two men—in the corridor where you are, and I asked them if they were the police and they said they were, mein Herr. I was a little surprised that I did not know either of them, mein Herr, and they said that, as the crime had been committed in France, French detectives had been sent to investigate it, mein Herr. So I left them to it and they have not long been gone, mein Herr, perhaps a half hour. You will have missed them in the station."

"No doubt," said Cournand, "no doubt. In order that, if I should meet them, I may recognize them at once, can you describe them at all?"

"Difficult," said the man, fingering his chin.

"No idea what they looked like?"

"*Ach*, yes, they looked like detectives. They wore felt hats and raincoats and had ordinary faces, mein Herr."

"Thank you," said Cournand, and straightened up from the window.

"Your criminals," said Virolet, "are regrettably quick off the mark."

"They were probably leaning against the door of the box while you were telephoning to me," said Cournand.

"Gentleman," said Hambledon, "assuming that our—er—precursors were again unlucky in their search, do you think it possible that they will now proceed to ransack Herr Bastien's flat or whatever he lived in?"

"A flat," said Cournand, leading the way across the tracks to the station at such a pace that the railway man who had been appointed to lead them was reduced to trotting behind, "a flat in Sandgrubenstrasse which is across the river. I will call for a police car."

"Has he," asked Hambledon, "any staff in the flat?"

"An elderly housekeeper who looked after Bastien and a niece of hers to look after the housekeeper, a country girl, not too bright. Well, here we are safely off those damned rail tracks. Just a minute while I ring for a car." Cournand entered a telephone box and Hambledon turned to Virolet.

"It occurs to me that I am intruding upon a matter which is no business of mine," he said. "It was very good of you and Herr Cournand to let me see so much. I ought to——"

"Are you, then, no longer interested in this enquiry?" interrupted Virolet. "You are on holiday and I am spoiling the start for you?"

"Not at all," said Hambledon, whose ruling passion was curiosity. "I am most interested, truly, and I should like above all things to see if anything has happened at the flat. It is only that I have no *locus standi*, no right to be with you."

"That is easily arranged," said Virolet. "If it will ease your conscience and legalize your presence, I can always arrest you as a suspect. Eh, Cournand?"

"What?"

"Monsieur Hambledon suffers from a feeling that he has no right to be with us."

"No right? Nonsense. In view of the fact that this case appears to involve international relations—Bastien went to France, didn't he—I shall call upon a representative of Britain to assist us in our enquiries. Or shall I enrol you as a special constable?"

"So long as I do not intrude," said Hambledon——

"*Quatsch*," said the Swiss. "Let us walk outside, the car will be here in a moment—here it comes."

They crossed the Rhine at the Wettstein Bridge and almost at once turned into a wide street.

"It is along here, a turning to the left," said Cournand. "It is a block of flats, not very new but comfortable. Do not drive up to the entrance," he added to the driver. "Take the nearest turning this side and we will walk on."

The car turned left into Sandgrubenstrasse, passed along it for a short distance, turned right into a quiet street, and stopped.

"Now," said Cournand, and hurried along to the entrance, a rather dull hall with a lift at the far end. There was no porter and they took themselves up to the third floor. "I have been here before," said Cournand. "Bastien used to have little parties sometimes. Stag parties," he added firmly, and rang the bell. The door was opened by an old woman, bent and frail, but with bright intelligent eyes.

"Good morning," said Cournand gently. "Do you remember me? Cournand, of the police. May we come in?"

"Certainly, Herr Cournand, but Herr Bastien is not at home. He is always travelling, as you know; he went away only yesterday all in a hurry as usual."

"May we go into the sitting room?" asked Cournand, leading the way. "Did he tell you where he was going, meine Frau?"

"He said he might be going to England. Yes, yes, it was to England that he was going. He had been there before, you know, many times before."

"Yes, I know," said Cournand, and there was a silence.

"Is there anything the matter? I am sure there is something the matter—is he ill?"

Come and sit down a moment, meine Frau," said Cournand, and led her to Bastien's armchair.

"He is ill, where is he? Tell me where he is."

"I am sorry," said Cournand, "very sorry to have to bring you bad news."

She looked piteously at him.

"He cannot be dead. It is not possible that he should be dead."

Hambledon and Virolet strolled across to the window. Arnoux had been left in the hall.

"He was——I looked after him when he was a little boy. I was his nurse. Yes, yes, when he was three years old I came to look after him."

No one spoke and after a moment she rose unsteadily to her feet and went sobbing out of the room.

"How I detest this kind of thing!" said Cournand violently "Damn all murderers!"

CHAPTER III

Tape Recorder

"At least," said Hambledon, "we have arrived before the other party this time. That is, I suppose so?"

"Since the place is not wrecked," agreed Cournand sourly, "but I will make sure." He strode to the door, which the housekeeper had closed after her, and opened it quietly. Outside there was a wide straight passage floored with small coloured tiles in patterns; there were three doors upon either side and, at the opposite end, the front door; the large room they were in took up the whole width of the flat. The middle door on their left was open and a girl was standing there leaning against the doorpost. She was short and square with thick arms and legs, hair which was really the colour of gold and was wound round her head in thick plaits, pink cheeks and very blue eyes, and a wide mouth which was never quite shut. She did not notice that the sitting-room door had opened; she was looking away from it towards the front door where Arnoux was standing, very stiff and upright, gazing earnestly at a framed model of a Dutch kitchen which hung on the wall in front of him. His round face was calm and composed but his ears were scarlet. They both held their poses unmoving; one would have said that they were figures in a picture. Cournand moved forward; the girl looked round and saw him and uttered a squeak like a mouse's.

"Here," said Cournand, "you, what's your name? I forget."

"Rosa, mein Herr, Rosa, if it please you."

"Rosa, has any man called here earlier this morning? Or possibly two men?"

"Two men, mein Herr, please."

"Strangers?"

"Oh no, mein Herr. One was the milkman and the other the postman."

"I see. Nobody else?"

"Oh no, mein Herr. But the baker will be here presently."

"Thank you," said Cournand, and went back to the sitting room. Virolet, who had been looking along the passage, crooked his finger and Arnoux, as one released from a spell, came to life and shot past the kitchen door into the sitting room, closing the door firmly behind him.

"My boy," said Virolet unkindly, "do your ears pain you?"

"No, monsieur, thank you," said Arnoux woodenly.

"They look inflamed."

"Tell me," said Hambledon, "what did she say to you?"

"Nothing, monsieur. Not a word."

"What? Just stood there and stared?"

"Precisely, monsieur."

"Since no one else has searched this place," said Cournand, "I think that we had better do so."

"May we help you?" asked Virolet.

"Please. I will take the desk if you will look elsewhere. They will only be put away somewhere if they are here at all, or casually concealed. No need to wreck the place."

Hambledon looked round the room. It was quite true that Bastien had taken to making ship models for, in spite of what he had said, there was one on the top shelf of a bookcase, another on the mantelpiece, and a third in course of construction on a table in the window. Virolet started on the bookcase, taking out each book, looking behind it, shaking it with the pages open downwards, and putting it back. He was incredibly quick. Arnoux began on the furniture; comfortable padded chairs in which an envelope might have been pushed down between seat and arm or slipped into a loose corner of the webbing covering the bottom. He unearthed a number of odd coins, a small pocket-knife and other trifles, but nothing for which anyone would endanger his life. He went on to the cupboards, of which there were several, a gramophone cabinet full of records——

Cournand at the desk seemed to be finding a great deal to interest him; muttered comments of surprise, annoyance, or satisfaction escaped him at intervals much as a terrier, digging in a bank, growls or squeaks as he labours.

Hambledon turned his attention to the finished models, but there was nowhere on them where a man could hide a sixpence. The unfinished one in the window was larger; perhaps this was one which poor Bastien might have intended to sail. The deck had not been secured. Hambledon lifted it off with careful fingers and found that the hull had been beautifully made with floor timbers and ribs, crossbeams and stringers, but it was quite empty. Bastien's toolbox was represented by the tabledrawer, and here again there was nothing incongruous. Also on the table was an electric table lamp, in the form of a candlestick, standing on a small attaché case, and Hambledon's interest awoke again as he noticed that the case had a flap on one side. He lifted off the heavy lamp and opened the case.

"Found something?" asked Virolet.

"A tape recorder," said Hambledon.

The tape had been run out; he set it to wind back and stood watching it while the spools whined round. What use would a free-lance journalist have for a tape recorder? Presumably to record conversations; Bastien was not likely to record his articles and send them out to be typed. His typewriter was on the desk. Tape recorders will preserve whole conversations without the speakers' knowledge if the microphone is concealed. The tape ran out and the end flicked tiresomely round the spool; Hambledon stopped it, threaded it back, and started it again.

There was silence for a moment or two and then, quite suddenly, the clatter and babble of a restaurant in the background and, more immediately, the small noises of chairs being moved and rustling sounds. Then a deferential voice saying: "Here is the menu. What will the herren be pleased to take?"

There followed a short discussion about food. Soup, yes? *Potage paysanne, bouillabaisse, soupe aux choux?* They made their different choices and the waiter repeated the orders.

"And to follow? Fish? The trout is very good. Or meat? There is veal or mutton——"

"What about your speciality? Tripe sausage from Angoulème——"

"Certainly, mein Herr. Three——"

"No," said another voice, "not for me. Far too rich. I should suffer——"

"What is all this?" asked Cournand. "A record of a dinner party?"

"Heaven knows," said Hambledon. "I am wondering why he took the trouble to record it."

"Somebody will make a speech," suggested Virolet.

"At the beginning of a dinner?" objected Cournand.

"Or sing a song," said Virolet. "Or play a vio——"

"Listen," said Hambledon urgently. The ordering had been completed and presumably the waiter had gone away because a confidential voice began to speak, very low but so close that every murmur was plainly audible; one could almost see the speaker leaning across the table.

"Tell us about the scheme now, Eugene, before he comes b-back. Then we can all think it over and if there are any questions to ask, there will be time to ask them."

Another voice answered just as quietly, a crisp voice, much more incisive.

"Very well. Today is Wednesday. On Friday night a Frenchman is coming from Paris to meet that Russian, Medeski, who is staying at the Drei Adlern." Cournand sat up abruptly. "The Frenchman is bringing the details of the latest American guided missile—flying bombs to you, Erich——"

"No, no," said Erich in a ponderous voice. "A rocket, of course, a guided rocket controllable either from the ground or from a piloted——"

"For heaven's sake!" broke in the incisive voice, presumably Eugene's. "Not a lecture just now, please. The Frenchman brings the papers, the Russian brings the money, and we are to get both."

"B-both," said the first speaker, who stuttered on certain consonants.

"Certainly. Both. Money is always useful and as for the dope about the rocket, the boss will sell it to the Russians again. The boss knows exactly what has been arranged. They will meet on Friday night."

"At the Drei Adlern?" That was Erich again, one who intended to see his way plainly, step by step.

"No, heavens no. Would that Frenchman go openly to a good hotel like that? He might be recognized. No. They are meeting in a room at the back of a café in Bergsteiger Strasse, a little place where the railway men go. There's an alley goes down beside the café, and the room has a side door to the alley."

"I know the p-place," said the stutterer. "It is where the b-blasted Reds m-meet. The café is called Der Schwartzhund."

"That's right. It isn't far from the station, so the Frenchman can catch the night train to Paris at half past twenty-two hours. The meeting—here comes our soup."

The waiter could be heard delivering different kinds of soup to the right recipients, and Cournand took the opportunity to remark that he knew that café. The Angoulême sausages were their trade-mark, as one might say; they were always——

"What time is the m-meeting?" asked the stutterer.

"At twenty-two hours. There will be Medeski and the Frenchman and Medeski's bodyguard, that is all. Now listen."

"We had b-better have our soup, or the waiter will notice."

"Short interval for soup," said Virolet.

"Evidently," said Hambledon, listening.

Eugene began again. "The bodyguard will be outside the door. Erich and I will silence him. Then I go in and get the stuff. There may be shooting. When I come out I shall be running hard towards the station; if I am stopped I am running to catch a train, the one for Olten at thirty-seven minutes past twenty-two. I already have the return half of a ticket to Olten. All clear so far? Good. Now go back to the alley down the side of the café. Paulus knows it; it is only a footpath between buildings and it runs through to the Karolinenstrasse. You know, Paulus? Good. There is a doorway halfway along on the left as you come from the café, a nice deep doorway."

"It is not used now," said Paulus; "it is fastened up. The m-maids used to slip out."

"All the better. Let us finish our soup and have the next course."

Spoons and plates clattered together; that would be the waiter clearing the first course. He brought the meat course and there was some desultory conversation at the table while it was being served.

"Do you know any of these men, Herr Cournand?" asked Hambledon. "It sounds as though the stuttering Paulus is a local man; he knows that district very well."

"I do know something," said Cournand; "I'll tell you when this is done. Eugene conveys nothing particularly sinister and there are hundreds of Erichs. I'll tell you this much right away; Paulus waited in that doorway they are talking about!"

"What——" began Virolet, but Hambledon shot out a hand and stopped him.

"This doorway," prompted Erich.

"If I am running for my train and should by chance be stopped, I can't afford to have anything on me. Paulus, you will stand in the doorway. When you hear me come running, flap a white handkerchief and I shall know it's you. I will hand you the goods as I go by, and then you can stroll off all calm and casual. Erich will have gone the other way, back into Bergsteiger Strasse and we'll all meet at Anna's. All clear?"

"Let me recapitulate," said the thick voice of Erich. "You and I go to the side door and lay out the bodyguard while Paulus waits in the doorway further on. Then you go in and get the stuff and come out again. You will have money and papers. You give me the money and I go back the way we came and round to Anna's. You go the other way past Paulus, give him the papers, and go straight on. Paulus also goes to Anna's and so do you if you are not pursued. That is correct, is it not?"

There was a short silence filled only with restaurant noise, and Erich repeated his question with a perceptibly harder tone in his voice. "That is correct, is it not?"

"Yes, of course," said Eugene's clearer voice. "I am sorry, I was thinking about weapons. I must have a gun when I enter that room though I don't like the noise. A silencer makes a gun so bulky."

"For the bodyguard," said Erich, "a knife."

"Certainly. Of course. But it would not do inside. Two of them and probably the other side of a table——"

"If the p-proprietor of the café would turn on his wireless it would dr——"

The tape ran off the first spool and the end spun round the second one with an audible flick every time it passed the end of the sound head; Hambledon put out his hand and stopped the mechanism.

"It becomes clear," said Virolet. "Bastien got those papers by a trick and the trick——"

"Consisted," interrupted Cournand, "in Bastien's walking up to a policeman on his beat in the Karolinenstrasse and saying: 'I believe the Lucerne police have been asking for Paulus Caron, haven't they? Armed robbery, I believe? He is down the Bergsteiger Gässlein over there, standing in a doorway. Go and look.' So my man went and looked. It is very dark in that alley, so he shone his torch on the doorway, and Paulus kicked it out of his hand and ran for it."

"Which way?" asked Hambledon and Virolet with one voice.

"Towards the Karolinenstrasse, away from his friends. My man ran after him, naturally, and they both passed Bastien waiting at the end of the alley for what should come."

"Then, no doubt, Bastien took Paulus's place in the doorway," said Virolet, "until he heard another set of running feet coming up from the café end——"

"Whereupon he gracefully flourished his white handkerchief, and Eugene kindly handed over the papers as he whizzed past," said Hambledon. "After which, Bastien walked quietly to the station and caught the next train to Calais for England. I wonder——"

"Tell me, Cournand," said Virolet, "what happened in that room at the back of the café?"

"I only know what we found," said Cournand, "we of the police, I mean. One dead man who had been knifed outside the door and his body dragged inside, and one dead Frenchman with a bullet in his brain."

"Who was the Frenchman?" asked Virolet and Cournand hesitated.

"I am sorry," he said at last, "I must not tell you. I have been commanded to secrecy. I will never utter that name."

"But," persisted Virolet, "somebody must be missing or have died suddenly——" his voice tailed off.

"He certainly died suddenly," agreed Cournand.

"Of a shooting accident—it cannot be he!—on a country estate near Rheims yesterday—oh, no. Not that man. They were shooting rooks with a rifle and——"

"And there will be a beautiful State funeral," said Cournand sarcastically. "That will be enough about him. We, of course, have only one corpse to deal with, and as nobody knows who he is, that will not give us much trouble. As for Comrade Medeski at the Drei Adlern, we know all about him. He is on the staff of the Russian Embassy at Berne."

"Has he gone back there," asked Virolet, "or is he still here?"

"I don't know but of course it is only to ask. He must be seriously annoyed, eh?"

"I'll tell you of some other people who will be seriously annoyed also," said Hambledon. "If Medeski has not returned, complete with papers, to the fold at Berne, his countrymen will be after him, won't they?"

"While Medeski is after Eugene and his friends——" said Cournand.

"Who in their turn ran vigorously after Monsieur Bastien," said Virolet. "So vigorously that they caught up with him last night in the Calais-Basle express. I wonder who they are running after now?"

"He was going to England," said Hambledon. "He told his housekeeper so and it seems to be true, since he was certainly at Calais. I wonder why he turned back.

"I expect they turned him back," said Cournand. "Or he saw them waiting for him near the gangway and thought he had given them the slip by coming straight back."

" 'They'?" said Hambledon.

"Oh, not Eugene in person," said Cournand. "You see, it would take time, would it not, to realize what had happened? Paulus ran for it and my man after him——"

"Did he catch him?" asked Hambledon.

"Unfortunately, no. My man rang up the station and reported it. Soon after that the proprietor of Der Schwartzhund rang us up to say that there were two dead men in his little back room and would we come and clear away. When we found out who and what they were, of course we were more interested than ever in the running Paulus though, at the time, it might just possibly thave been coincidence. Well, after a while Paulus makes his way back to Anna's and they compare notes. Erich has got the money all right, and Paulus assumes that Eugene has still got the papers. 'I wasn't there,' he says, 'I had to run for it. Who did you give the p-papers to?' Eugene says somebody flapped a handkerchief as arranged and he naturally assumed it was Paulus. 'Who put the cop on to you?' asks Eugene. 'Wasn't there anyone about?' 'There was that newshawk B-Bastien,' says Paulus. 'I've seen him b-before.' So then they contact the boss. I wish I knew who he is, and I only hope he was nice about it. Don't you? By this time it was probably the small hours and Bastien in the Calais train passing through Strasbourg——"

"How did they know that?" asked Hambledon.

"Oh, somebody saw him and reported it when asked if anyone had seen Bastien. He was very well known."

"And they'd have somebody hanging round the station that night," said Virolet, "in case Eugene wanted help or to check on the Frenchman. That traitor," snarled Virolet, "may he rot in hell!"

"Calm yourself," said Cournand soberly. "I should say that he is already there. From death to hell is a short road for traitors, in my belief. Well, then the boss rings up a friend in Calais and says Bastien is not to reach England with his papers; they are to be taken off him. You, Herr Hambledon, saw that friend."

"Yes," said Hambledon, "yes. Dear Pierre. Perhaps your police, Monsieur Virolet, have gathered him in by now. By the way, didn't you admire the firm way in which Erich arranged to receive the money. So obviously sensible too; even Eugene didn't argue the point."

"One wonders," said Virolet, "what would have become of the money if either Paulus or Eugene had kept it."

"We don't know," pointed out Cournand, "that Erich didn't go off with it. I should not think so, myself; he knows his friends too well. But it would be a good sum, would it not?"

"It would not be—how do you say? Food for the fowls?" said Virolet.

"One last point," said Hambledon. "Anna."

"I shall not neglect Anna," said Cournand. "If it's a sort of pet name for a club or an inn, my police may know it. Of course, she may be merely an aunt."

"Some aunt," said Hambledon.

"Bastien," said Virolet, "would have been better advised to travel to London by air. I wonder he did not."

"It is possible that he could not get a seat," said Cournand; "they are heavily booked in the holiday season. Well, I think we have done all we can here. The next step is to go to the Café Angoulème. Herr Hambledon, do you accompany us?"

"Thank you," said Hambledon. "I should like very much to come with you, if I may. For one thing, I want to know how Bastien managed to conceal or disguise a microphone so that none of the three noticed it. It sounded as though it must have been on the table; when they leaned forward and spoke quietly they seemed to be whispering into it. Damn it, one could hear them breathing."

They went out together and found the girl Rosa again standing by the kitchen door, and her eyes fell upon Arnoux who retired behind Hambledon.

"Rosa," said Cournand, "has anyone else called?"

"Only the man from the telephone company, mein Herr, to inspect the telephone."

"What did you tell him?"

"That the police were here, mein Herr. He said that in that case he would call back later."

"Excuse me one moment," said Cournand, and went back to the telephone on Bastien's desk. They heard him talking to the telephone company and a moment later he returned.

"No?" said Hambledon.

"No, of course not. I shall put a man in here, but I don't think he will come back. He will know that if there was anything to find we should have found it."

"The tape recorder?" asked Hambledon.

"I have it, monsieur," said Arnoux. "Monsieur Cournand wants to have it at his office, so I brought it away."

"Unless," said Virolet, "you would rather stay here on guard? Let me take it from you."

"No thank you, monsieur," said Arnoux emphatically.

CHAPTER IV

Taxi!

The Café d'Angoulème was of the usual Continental type; small
tables with clean checked tablecloths stood, with freshly painted
chairs, on the pavement outside, and a neat menu card in a
shining brass frame hung upon one doorpost. Clean white curtains draped the windows; the walls inside had been newly
decorated and the floor was not yet dry from the daily scrubbing.
The room was of irregular shape with a number of deep alcoves.
Cournand led his way towards one of them and ordered coffee
when the waiter came. "And ask the manager to be so good as
to come and speak to us for a moment."

The place was almost empty at that hour, too late for
breakfast and too early for lunch; most of the waiters, still in
linen jackets, were laying tables, polishing already shining
glasses, and dusting already speckless chairs. Hambledon said
that it was a nice place and Cournand agreed with him. "I come
here sometimes," he added. "I probably shall again, but not to
talk secrets, no."

The manager came, a short fat man with gold-rimmed spec-
tacles and a gold watch chain across his black waistcoat.

"Good morning, Herr Cournand. One of my fellows says you
are so kind as to wish to speak to me."

Cournand said that that was so, yes, and asked the manager
if he knew Herr Bastien, the press correspondent.

"Certainly I do, certainly. Who does not? He comes here very often; not every day but whenever, I suppose, he is hungry in this vicinity. I have known him many years now."

"He was, you would say, a friend of yours?" asked Cournand.

"I hope I may so—you said 'was.' Has anything happened?"

"I am sorry," said Cournand. "He is dead."

"Dead? But he was here on—" the manager hesitated—"on Wednesday and again on Thursday. He seemed quite well then. Was it, then, an accident?"

Cournand, with a look, transferred the question to Virolet who leaned forward.

"It is more startling than that, monsieur. Your poor friend has been murdered."

"Murdered! When?"

Virolet glanced at Hambledon, who picked up his cue.

"He was shot in the head, monsieur. I was there and saw it. He died almost at once. That was at two o'clock this morning."

The manager turned in his chair and looked absently across the room for a moment.

"I liked him," he said, and his jaw tightened.

"That being so," said Cournand briskly, "I think you can help us. Cast your mind back to the evening of Wednesday last. You had three men together in here to dinner that night, and I think Herr Bastien was interested in them."

The man started violently. "Herr Cournand, do not tell me—— I could not bear it if I were at all responsible——"

"What did you do?"

"It was irregular, I know, but I did not mean to do anything wrong——Herr Bastien was a man in whom I had the most profound confidence——"

"Begin at the beginning," said Cournand, "and tell us all about it. One moment."

A waiter came with the coffee which had been ordered, set it down and asked if there were anything else required.

"Yes," said the manager, "I will have a *fine*. A large one, from the bottle at the back of my shelf. Gentlemen will you join me? Five, Franz, all from the same bottle." He took his glasses off to wipe his forehead. "This has been a horrid shock, gentlemen. I am sure that for weeks to come I shall look up when the door opens, expecting to see him. For it is so with an unexpected death; it is not that one thinks of it continually but that one forgets, and so the tragedy happens over and over again."

"That is very true," said Hambledon. The brandy came; the manager sipped his and the colour came back to his face.

"It was like this," he said. "Herr Bastien came to me on Wednesday morning at about this time—no, a little earlier, the tables had not been laid—and said that three men would be coming to dinner that night. He described them to me so that I could not fail to recognize them. He said that they were evil men planning an evil deed and if he could get evidence against them he could act against them, but he must have evidence. I—I am sorry—I did not take him too seriously; I asked if he wished to disguise himself as a waiter. He laughed and said heaven forbid, he would certainly upset the soup all over them. Besides, he said, they probably knew him by sight. Then he became serious and said that it was a very grave matter and I must help him. All he wanted to do was to put a lamp, which he brought with him, on a certain table, the one in that far alcove. It backs onto the staff cloakrooms; there is only a wooden partition though you would not think so to look at it. This lamp, which he took out of a suitcase, was like mine; they are a common pattern but this one had a microphone in it, or so he told me. When the waiter switched on the table lamp—they are only lit when the tables are in use—he would switch on the microphone also. The Herr understands? Myself, I know nothing of these matters; it looked like an ordinary lamp to me. Then he bored a small hole through the partition low down, near the floor, and drew the wire from the lamp through it into the staff cloakroom behind. Later in the day, in the evening, he came with a small attaché case and went into the cloakroom with it. He watched from behind the screen there till he saw these men come in and then rushed into the cloakroom. I myself showed them to their table. That is all I know, gentlemen. I did not attempt to hear anything of what they said——"

"No need," said Cournand. "Can you describe them?"

The manager did so. They were all men in the middle thirties; one was tall, slim, and well spoken, another was dark and thick-set, probably a German, the third was pale to the point of being colourless; he had a slight impediment in his speech. The manager added further details about their appearance and Arnoux noted them all down. "My waiter, Franz, the one who brought the coffee just now, he waited upon them. Perhaps he can tell you more about them."

"Thank you, I will ask him," said Cournand. "One more question, if you will forgive me. Did Herr Bastien tell you how he got on the track of these people?"

"I asked him that. I said, 'How the devil do you get hold of all these dreadful stories, eh?' He only laughed and said that he had many friends who talked to him. It was true, gentlemen; he had so many people who told him things—bits of broken stories—he told me once, which he spent his days fitting together."

"Yes," said Cournand, "yes. Have you," he turned to Hambledon and Virolet, "any more questions before we cease to waste this gentleman's whole morning for him?"

Virolet shook his head and Hambledon said, "One thing only. If we might see one of your table lamps?"

One was brought; it was of the familiar Corinthian column pattern with a switch on the wide and heavy base and a silk shade over the electric bulb. It was the duplicate of that which Hambledon had lifted off the tape recorder in Bastien's flat.

"Thank you," said Hambledon, and the lamp was solemnly borne away again.

"I have remembered something else the Herr Bastien said," added the manager. "He spoke, as I told you, of an evil deed, and I asked him whether there would be any reward to make a little nest egg for his old age—I was still not taking the matter very seriously—and he said not in money, no, but as a journalist's scoop, ah! If he could pull it off he would, he said, retire on his laurels and build little ships. You have seen his little ships? Yes. I asked if I should read about it in our papers and he said in all the papers of the civilized world starting with the London *Times,* that great paper. Ah, well. Is there any matter in which I can serve you further, gentleman? If you would excuse me, then, there is one of our suppliers waiting to see me. I am always here if you want me, gentlemen."

The manager trotted away. Cournand said he thought that when they had got any extra information the waiter Franz might have noticed or overheard, that would conclude the usefulness of the Café d'Angoulème. Virolet suggested that Arnoux could take Franz's statement if that would be any help to Monsieur Cournand, and Cournand answered that in view of the probability that the papers on his desk were now piled up till they touched the ceiling, he would be much obliged. The four men got up from the table as Hambledon said that there was one curious point which emerged, was there not? The Herr Bastien had known beforehand of a murderous affray being planned for the back room of Der Schwartzhund and had done absolutely nothing whatever to prevent or even hinder it.

"In view of the personalities involved," snarled Virolet, "on both sides, no doubt he thought that they would all be much better dead. All of them, and I agree with him. If I had known beforehand what Bastien knew, I should have encouraged the affair with all the resources at my disposal. Eh, Cournand?"

"It is easily seen," said Cournand, "that this is not your city. Nevertheless, there is something in what you say. Well now, Herr Hambledon, what would you like to do?"

Hambledon said that he thought he would now pursue his journey. There was a train to Innsbruck at about fourteen hours; he would have lunch and go by that.

"Do not forget your rucksack," said Virolet. "When you go striding over those mountains you will need it, will you not? Is that all the luggage you have?"

"There are a couple of suitcases also, but I registered them straight through to Seefeld."

Hambledon's train drew into Innsbruck soon after half past nine that night; he collected his gear, presented his roll of magazines to a fellow traveller who would not reach Vienna until breakfast time the following morning, and stepped down onto the platform.

"I suppose," he said, accosting a passing porter, "that the last train to Seefeld is already gone."

"Oh yes, mein Herr, two hours ago. Will the Herr stay in the town tonight? There is a train at five-fifteen tomorrow——"

"*Pfui!*" said Hambledon violently.

"And another just after eight," said the porter hurriedly. "And numerous others later, of course."

Hambledon hesitated, for he was in that state of fatigue when it seems desirable to press on to one's final destination at all costs rather than to break the interminable journey again. He asked how far it was to Seefeld and learned that it was only about fifteen miles.

"I think I'll hire a taxi," he said. "No doubt there are plenty of garages here who will be willing to drive me to Seefeld?"

"Certainly, mein Herr. Also there are taxis waiting outside the station entrance," said the porter, pointing it out. "Shall I call one up for the Herr?"

"Don't bother," said Hambledon, "thank you. No doubt I shall find one." He turned to go and a voice spoke at his shoulder.

"With excuses," it said, "for addressing the Herr unasked——"

Hambledon looked around. There was a young man at his elbow with a cheerful and apologetic expression.

"I could not avoid hearing what the Herr said to the porter," said the young man. "Asking pardon, I am myself a taxi driver and I have to go to Seefeld empty tonight to pick up a fare to drive back here, to Innsbruck. If the Herr would care to come in my car it would not cost him so much as it otherwise would; also it will pay me rather better—excuse me! It is, of course, entirely as the Herr wishes."

"Thank you——" began Hambledon.

"Unless the Herr wishes to start at once," said the young man. "I have, unfortunately, a couple of hire runs to do first."

"I don't in the least wish to start at once," said Hambledon. "On the contrary, I want a meal before I go. When were you thinking of starting?"

The young man glanced up at the clock. "In an hour's time, if that will suit the Herr? At a quarter before twenty-three hours?"

"Very good," said Hambledon. "I will meet you at the station entrance, here, in an hour's time," at which the young man grinned, saluted, and hurried away.

Hambledon, tired to aching point, hungry and thirsty—for there is no restaurant car on that train—stumbled over uneven platforms in the fading light and out to the dusty road outside. He checked his rucksack and walked on. He had not been to Innsbruck since long before the war; towards the end of it the station had been bombed or shelled, or both, and he did not recognize what he saw outside, a large open space upon the far side of which strings of little tramcars crawled jerkily along. On his right there were hoardings hiding he knew not what, on his left an enormous hole in the ground which reminded him of the gaping cellars of Cologne, and the road upon which he walked was of cobblestones alternated with patches of soft dust. Ahead, however, things looked better; the wide Salurner Strasse seemed to be intact, the street lamps were pricking the violet dusk with points of gold, somewhere ahead there were strings of coloured lights, and from an open window high above him there came the sound of an orchestra playing Viennese waltzes. Hambledon's spirits rose and he turned into the Hochhaus café's humming to himself.

He came out, nearly an hour later, more cheerful still. Only a fifteen-mile run in a presumably comfortable car lay between him and journey's end; another half hour or a little more and he could be at rest in a place which did not sway, bump, or rattle, where he could have a bath, go to bed and stay there all night. Marvellous.

When he reached the station he found his driver already there, sitting at the wheel of a Citroën saloon, not very new but clean and well cared for; he saw Hambledon coming and got out to open the door for him. Hambledon thought for a moment that he had seen the man's face before but it was probably fancy; he had seen so many faces. A chance resemblance.

"Just a moment," said Hambledon. "I have some things in the cloakroom. I will get them."

"But of course," said the driver. "Stupid of me," and he walked with Hambledon to the left-luggage office which is close by the main door. Hambledon carried his own coat and stick and the driver burdened himself with the rucksack.

"Is this, then, all the luggage? It is easily seen that the Herr is an experienced traveller; he travels light."

"You don't mind going off into the wilds at this time of night?"

The driver laughed. "It is not so late to our way of thinking, nor so very far, mein Herr. Besides, it is my livelihood, so why should I complain? It is true that the road is not of the best but I am used to it."

"Bad surface?"

"Oh no, mein Herr. It is the gradient; the road up to Seefeld is the second steepest hill in all the Tyrol. Parts of it are one-in-four."

"Indeed," said Hambledon, getting into the rear seat. "I hope this car has a good engine."

"Let the Herr have no misgivings. We shall go slowly in places, but we shall continue to go." The driver shut the door, put Hambledon's rucksack on the front seat beside his own, and got in himself. The car turned and drove away as Hambledon settled down comfortably and lit a cigarette. They passed through a number of lighted streets, crossed a bridge over the turbulent Inn, and soon afterwards turned left onto the main road to the Arlberg Pass and Switzerland. The lights of the town fell behind, the road was wide and good, and the car hummed along until the driver slowed at Zirl for the turn to Seefeld. Hambledon, who was half asleep, roused up at this and saw that the road was narrower and winding; a little further on the lights of the car illuminated a notice board. The something-or-other Catgut Factory, it said. Hambledon remembered that Mittenwald, famous for violins, was only just over the German frontier a few miles ahead and murmured, "Poor pussy. But it's all synthetic these days."

Trees overhung the road which started to rise, the car laboured, and the driver changed gears. Up and up, round sharp bends with a wall of rock on their left and what looked like illimitable depths on the right, treetops close to the road as the head lamps swung for another bend, tiny points of light in the valley below. The driver was changing gears all the time, down to second, down to bottom, up for an easier stretch, down again. At a point where the road seemed by comparison almost level, the driver pulled the car in to the side of the road, stopped, got out, and came to the rear door on the right. Hambledon leaned forward as the door opened and began, "Are you in trouble? Can I do——" and stopped abruptly.

The driver had a businesslike Lüger automatic in his hand, and it was levelled at Hambledon.

CHAPTER V

The Antique Shop

"What the devil," roared Hambledon, "is the meaning of this? Put that gun down."

"Get undressed," said the driver, and Hambledon did not believe his ears. The man must be mad.

"*What* did you say?"

"I said, get undressed. Take your clothes off."

"Don't be ridiculous," said Hambledon angrily. "Are you touting for a nudist colony, or what?"

"If you don't want a bullet through your head, do what you're bid! Take your clothes off. All of them, and drop them in the car."

Hambledon thought that he had never felt such a fool in his life, or so helpless. He began to take his coat off and the man snarled at him.

"Quicker than that! You're not idling into bed. Get on with it."

"If this were robbery," thought Hambledon, unbuttoning his waistcoat, "he wouldn't want my clothes, he'd want my wallet." A picture rose in his mind of Bastien's clothes on the floor of the sleeping compartment in the Basle express, with their seams slit and the lining torn out, and a possible explanation presented itself. He considered saying, "If you're still looking for that infernal Frenchman's papers, I haven't got them," and desisted because he was not likely to be believed. This man was not one of the three who had dined round Bastien's candlestick at the

Café d'Angoulême; his voice did not resemble any of theirs, but someone might have travelled with Hambledon on the train to Innsbruck and pointed him out. There was Pierre who killed Bastien, there were the three men in Basle, and now this one. A biggish gang and widely dispersed.

"Now come out," said the man.

Hambledon drew himself up with as much dignity as is consistent with being mother-naked, and slid along the seat towards the open door. The man drew back to let him pass, unconsciously lowering his gun as he did so. Hambledon, now in the doorway, suddenly threw himself back and thrust violently with both bare feet against the man's chest. He was caught off guard, lost his hold on the door handle, and staggered back into the darkness.

The next moment there was a sliding sound, one awful yell, a series of crashing noises getting fainter and further below, and then total silence.

"Good God," said Hambledon, "I've pushed him over the edge." He sat with his head in both hands for a moment and then began hastily to scramble into his clothes again.

"After all," he concluded, "he asked for it."

When he was once more decently clothed, if rather inaccurately buttoned, he stood in the road and looked at the car.

"It seems a pity," he said, "but I think you'd better go over and join your master. With the driver's door open as a matter of corroborative detail. Much as I dislike the thought of humping this pack to Seefeld."

He took all his things out of the car, very careful to leave nothing behind which could suggest that the Citroën had had a passenger, then started the engine, turned the car across the road and let it run back without him. It hung on the edge for a moment, slid over and disappeared from sight but not, for what seemed a long time, from hearing.

"Noisy things, cars," said Hambledon.

He wriggled into his rucksack, slung his coat through the straps, picked up his stick, and proceeded to walk to Seefeld.

"I think this is one of the most unused roads I ever came along," he said to himself at the end of twenty minutes. "There hasn't been a car along since that one we met by the cat factory. Do all these people go to bed at ten?"

They do not, at least in that part of Austria. The reason why the road was so unfrequented was that, since it was not yet midnight, nobody had even begun to go home. One car came down the hill towards him, going to Innsbruck, so he made no attempt to stop it, and the travellers saw only a sight so common that they barely glanced at it, a hiker with a rucksack on his back plodding on, and on, and on. He stopped abruptly.

"I have seen that fellow's face before. He was hanging about Basle station when I came out with Virolet and Cournand. He looked at me then, I noticed it. I must have been half asleep not to know him again. Either that was his own car or he borrowed it from a friend. He knew where to get it."

He walked on.

"Well, that proves one thing. This attack was all part of the Bastien affair, and they think I have those infernal papers. I might put an advertisement in the *Continental Daily Mail:* T. E. Hambledon presents his compliments to the murderers of the late Herr Edouard Gilles Bastien and others and begs to assure them that he hasn't got their filthy papers and wouldn't touch them with a pair of tongs if he found them on the mat. He is on holiday and will be obliged if he may so continue.

The road wound up and up, past a long stretch of road work in progress and round a newly terraced hairpin bend. Above this Hambledon, pausing for a short rest, looked down upon the way he had come and saw a pair of headlights coming up from below, turning this way and that.

When the driver of this car in his turn negotiated the hairpin bend he saw in the beams of his lamps a rather disconsolate figure sitting on a lump of rock at the side of the road. The figure had one shoe off and was carefully and tenderly replacing its sock.

The car pulled up; the driver stuck his head out and asked if there was any trouble and, if so, could he help in any way. By giving a lift, for instance?

Hambledon, hurriedly replacing his shoe, limped across to the car and said that indeed a lift to Seefeld would fulfil all his immediate desires if the Herr was going that way?

"I am," said the driver. "Do get in." He leaned across to open the opposite door while Hambledon made his painful way round the bonnet.

"Thank you so much," said Hambledon, getting in and immediately removing his shoe again. "You know, this is all my own fault and I deserve it for being stupid. I am on holiday and hope to get some walking; like a fool I thought I would start by walking from Innsbruck to Seefeld and the first thing I do is to spring a blister."

"I thought you must be a newcomer to our mountains," said the driver, "when I saw that you were wearing shoes. And, incidentally, trousers. Stout boots and shorts are what you want."

"How right you are," said Hambledon. "*Lederhosen* are what I should like if I should not look too much like a tourist."

"*Herrgott*, no," said the driver. "Everybody wears them. I do myself," and he chuckled comfortably. *Lederhosen* are the short breeches made of soft leather which nine men out of ten in the mountainous districts of Central Europe wear as a matter of course; the point of the joke in this case was that the driver was one of the fattest men Hambledon had ever seen. He overflowed his seat, his face resembled the full moon, and his wrists were creased like a baby's; what he must look like in shorts Hambledon could not imagine. "I have them made for me," said the driver, and chuckled again. He spoke the German of Austria, not a country patois but the hard Austrian accent. Hambledon took him to be one of the local inhabitants.

"I hope I am not taking you out of your way," he said.

"Not in the least," said the driver.

"Do you live in Seefeld?"

"Oh, no. I live in Munich, if a man of my profession can be said to live anywhere but in his car. I am a traveller in musical instruments if you can call them that."

"Violins?" said Hambledon, thinking of Mittenwald.

The driver laughed aloud. "Nothing so high brow. Mouth organs are my horrid trade. Look, those are the lights of Seefeld ahead. Do you know where you want to go?"

"I have a room booked in a hotel," said Hambledon putting his shoe on again, "but I don't know exactly where the hotel is. If you would be so good as to put me down somewhere in the

middle of the town, I shall manage very well. What I want first
of all is a drink. Will you join me?"

"That is extraordinarily good of you but I won't, if you will
forgive me. I have been held up all day and I want to get in.
Please forgive me——"

"Of course," said Hambledon. "It was good of you to stop
for me and I am immensely grateful. I hope that we shall meet
again."

"I hope so, too," said the driver. "Keep you eyes open and
if you see something on the skyline that looks like a mountain,
only moving, it will be me. Look, here's the town square if that's
what they call it. I'll drop you at the Lamm—is that your hotel?
No? Never mind, it's a very nice one and you'll get a drink
there before you stagger on. Got all your gear? That's right—
not at all, a pleasure, believe me. *Auf wiedersehen.*"

He drove cheerfully away. Hambledon had the drink which
he felt he not only needed but deserved, and asked his way to
the Karwendelhof Hotel. Was it far? Only round there, across the
road and up the Bahnhofstrasse, at the end on the left. Oh no,
not far.

Nor was it. Hambledon walked up the short street, wide
enough to allow cars to be parked on the side opposite the shops;
one of the cars caught his attention, a saloon of which he remembered the number; it was the fat man's car. Hambledon was
mildly surprised, for he had somehow received the impression
that his benefactor was driving straight on through; in point of
fact, he had not actually said so. Probably he was staying in a
private house with friends; otherwise "I wonder if we're bound
for the same hotel" would have been a natural remark.

The Karwendelhof's illuminated sign pointed Hambledon's
way, and there came the sound of dance music to lighten his
step; if the fat man had been watching him then he would have
noticed that the limp had gone. It was a little after midnight
and there were a number of people about outside; in the entrance
hall also cheerful groups were discussing the day's doings or
making plans for the morrow. Hambledon went up to the reception desk and introduced himself.

"We expected you on the afternoon train," said the receptionist.

"We were beginning to wonder whether you had gone astray."

"I was tired of trains," said Hambledon, "and it was such a lovely day that I decided to walk. You want my passport, here it is."

"Thank you," said the receptionist, getting out the register and booking list from under the counter. "It is a long way from Innsbruck and up a very steep hill."

"I noticed your hill," laughed Hambledon. "In fact, I cheated and got a lift for the last few miles or I should have been later still. I did not want to arrive too late and find you had all gone to bed."

"You would have to be very late for that! Here is your key; you are on the third floor. I am sorry there is no lift as yet. I will come up and show you your room unless you would like a little something first. Have you had dinner?"

"I had something on the road, thank you. I think I will go straight up."

"You must be tired," said the receptionist sympathetically. The stairs were on the same side of the hall as the reception desk but masked from it by the wall. Hambledon went up a few steps and then had to wait for his guide who had been detained by a party of people who wanted to be called at seven. While Hambledon stood there he heard a voice he knew speaking at the reception desk to the tall dark girl who had taken the other's place.

"Can I have a single room, please?"

"You have not a room already booked?"

"Oh, no. No, I came in on the chance. I hope you can manage."

There was a short pause while, doubtless, records were being consulted. The fat man—perhaps his friends were out.

"There is a room vacant in the annex——"

"Where is that?"

"Just across the public gardens here; it is no distance."

"I would rather be in the hotel itself if that is possible." Another short pause.

"There is a vacant room on the top floor—it is rather small——"

"So long as the door is wide enough to admit me!"

The girl laughed softly. "May I have your passport, please? Or—oh, you are Austrian. Your identity papers——"

The receptionist dashed after Hambledon, apologizing, and led the way past two floors, halfway to the next, turned right up a few wide steps and along a passage.

"This is the Herr's room, the first door on this corridor. The room has a balcony, as you see. I hope the Herr will be comfortable. Is there anything else I can do?"

"No, thank you—well, yes, one thing. Did you happen to notice a very stout man who came to the reception desk while I was waiting for you?"

"I did see him, yes."

"Do you know who he is?"

"No, mein Herr. I did not recognize him."

"It doesn't matter," said Hambledon. "Actually, it was he who gave me the lift I told you about and I wondered what his name is."

"The Herr may see him in the morning."

"Most probably. Well, thank you very much."

Hambledon came down to breakfast not too early on a brilliantly sunny morning and found himself directed to a table in a wide window looking across at the Karwendel range of mountains which is the frontier with Germany. He sat looking contentedly at it, reflecting that snow in sunshine really does glitter, until his coffee and rolls came. Then he opened an Innsbruck paper to see whether last night's car crash had attracted any public attention. It was probably too soon for it to appear in the paper unless the wreck had been found very quickly— here it was, rather smeary and hurried-looking.

Fatality on the Seefeld Road near Leithen, said the headline, and went on:

There was a fatal accident on the road from Zirl to Seefeld last night when a saloon car went off the road on a sharp turn and fell some three hundred feet to the bed of a small stream. The accident was seen by a farm worker of Leithen who saw the lights of the car descend precipitously the abrupt declivity, turning round and over till extinguished with crashing sounds. He

*informed the police who reached the spot to find the driver
dead of multiple injuries.*

"So, I imagine, was the car," murmured Hambledon.

*The car, which had been stolen, was the property of Herr A. G.
Eisenschmidt, the well-known and esteemed antique dealer of
the Lieberstrasse, Innsbruck. It is thought that the dead man may
be a well-known criminal, and police enquiries are in progress.*

Hambledon thought this a little odd since the man had been
openly showing himself at the railway station at Innsbruck, but
of course the police may not have wanted him for anything just
then. Herr Eisenschmidt sounded as though he could not possibly be more respectable, though a dealer in antiques; perhaps
the car really was stolen, after all. It might be a good idea to
go down to Innsbruck by train and have a look at the esteemed
Herr Eisenschmidt. No time like the present; he would go today.

He finished the last crumb of roll and the last drop of coffee
and strolled through the hall to the reception desk to ask about
trains to Innsbruck. He was told that he had lost the four minutes
past nine train and that the next one was the ten forty-six, a
good train; it stopped nowhere before Innsbruck.

Everyone seemed to be talking about last night's accident and
the clerk was no exception. "Did the Herr see anything of the
dreadful crash on that road last night? It is in the paper."

"I was reading about it," said Tommy Hambledon. "No, he
must have been before me or after me. Before, I should think,
since the news is in the paper and I was pretty late. They do
not give the time when it happened."

"It was about half past twenty-three hours," said the clerk. "So
it is said, locally."

"Oh, then I was past by that time," said Tommy. "I had one
or two periods of rest, you know, coming up that hill. Now I
come to think of it, I believe I did hear a distant crash at some
point. I took it to be a tree falling."

He turned round and came face to face with the fat man who
was choosing picture post cards. What was more, he was actually
wearing *lederhosen* and a sports jacket.

"Oh, good morning," said Hambledon. "Glad to see you again. Are you staying here?"

"I shan't know until tonight. Are you?"

"Oh yes," said Hambledon, "yes, rather. By the way, my name's Hambledon."

"Mine is Lombard," said the fat man, paying for his cards. "Lucius Lombard. You must excuse me if I push off now. I overslept so I am late. See you tonight with any luck." He nodded, pushed open the swing door with his shoulder, and was gone.

Hambledon strolled across to the station, the yard of which adjoins the side of the Karwendelhof. He told himself that there was plenty of time to get his suitcase out of the customs shed, carry it across to the hotel, and return, but he argued with himself that there was no point in that at all since he would not want the things until he came back from Innsbruck and he would then be walking back to the hotel anyway, that it was very pleasant on that warm sunny platform with the cool air blowing down off the snows and plenty of countryfolk to talk to, and finally that at the moment he had no interest in luggage and did not propose to take any interest. When the train came in he climbed up into a carriage and enjoyed the run down, although they seemed to be going so fast that the telegraph poles whizzed past the windows like fence posts.

Herr Lucius Lombard, taking a rather nasty corner far too fast, thanked Heaven piously for the man who invented exhaust-brakes. He had told the truth when he had said that he was in a hurry; he had to be at Innsbruck station before Hambledon's train came in, and there were some important people to see before that.

Hambledon had not been in Innsbruck for a number of years except for his brief visit in search of dinner the night before. He looked about him when he came out of the station and saw no one whom he recognized. He walked away into the town and eventually found the Lieberstrasse.

It was a quiet street mainly of private houses but with half-a-dozen small but superior shops, one of which was an antique shop with the name A. G. Eisenschmidt above the single wide window. The shop door was on the right of the window and, next beyond the door, an alley ran down between the houses.

Tommy glanced into it in passing; it was wide enough for a car.

He stopped to look in the shopwindow which contained all the usual things: three or four small but good pieces of furniture including a lacquered corner cupboard, some rather miscellaneous cut glass and china, one bronze which was antique and two which certainly were not, and some trays full of oddments, such as snuffboxes, garnet jewellery, and one or two miniatures. There was also a set of carved ivory chessmen under a glass case. There was no doubt about the business being genuine, though for all the local colour it contained it might have been in Kensington. Hambledon opened the door and went in; when an old man came forward to serve him he was looking at intaglio seals in a tray.

The old man was very old indeed. Tommy looked at him with respect and said to himself, "Eighty if he's a day. Probably more." Aloud he said, "You have some very nice seals here."

"Some of them are," said the old man in a high thin voice, "but they are of various periods, as the Herr sees. Some of the heraldic ones are of very fine workmanship." The thin old fingers slid among the tiny blocks of chalcedony and agate. "Here is a good one. The arms are those of the Welser family. But I have at present no seals in stock which date back to classical times."

"Immutably honest," said Hambledon to himself, and added, "You are yourself the Herr Eisenschmidt?"

"I am, yes."

Hambledon put down the seal of the Welser family.

"Then, mein Herr, I think it was your car which was stolen last night and which subsequently came to grief on the Seefeld road?"

"Not my personal car," said Eisenschmidt. "I have no private car of my own since I myself no longer drive, mein Herr." Tommy thought that in such country it was just as well. "The car belongs to the business, that is, to the proprietors."

"But are you not the proprietor? Your name——"

"Is still over the window, yes, and the business is still run in my name, but I no longer own it. I did at one time, yes, and my father before me, but there were difficulties and I had to sell. So now I am only the salesman, but I am still here and so is the name. I am very fortunate, mein Herr; also the young men who own it are often glad of my advice as a buyer; yes, yes, as a buyer. This business needs an apprenticeship of a lifetime and still there is much to learn."

"I do not doubt it. I am myself," said Hambledon with simple pride, "a journalist by profession. I am on the staff of the *Algemeen Handelsblad* of Amsterdam. I am on holiday in this district and I thought that an account of this car being stolen by a famous criminal who came to a bad end almost in the act would make a little story for my paper, you understand?"

"I understand very well," said the old man, laughing. "One may be on holiday, but the work is still the life, is it not? When I was young and used to take my holidays in Venice, in Rome, in Zurich, I spent my days drifting from one antique shop to another."

"Do you think," said Hambledon, "that I might see the proprietor for a few minutes—does he live in Innsbruck? What is his name?"

"Norz, mein Herr, Gustav Norz, and he lives on the first floor over this shop. It is a very nice flat and has a private entrance. Once I used to live there myself, but it is too large for me now. Excuse me, I will ring up and ask if he will see you. He may not be at home."

The old gentleman ambled away to the back of the shop and could be heard using a house telephone of the type on which one vigorously winds a handle to ring the bell. A moment later he was asking whether Herr Norz would receive a journalist from Amsterdam about the stolen car. Oh no; only for a few minutes. Oh no; on the contrary, very pleasant and gentlemanly —in a lowered voice still audible to Tommy's quick ears.

He came back and said that Herr Norz would receive the Herr and was sending his own servant down to show him up. The next minute there came the sound of a key turning in a lock and a door opened at the back of the shop.

"Up the stairs, if you please," said the manservant.

Hambledon walked slowly up a narrow flight of stairs and, as he did so, heard the key turned again in the door behind him.

CHAPTER VI

The Carpet

The manservant was a large raw-boned young man with a sullen expression and hands like hams. Tommy thought him an odd type to be a house servant; he looked more nearly like a race-course tough, but perhaps Norz liked them like that. Hambledon was shown into a large and pleasant sitting room looking out on the street; the servant crossed it, tapped at a door on the further side, and entered. There was a murmur of voices and the man came back.

"What name, please?"

"Hambledon, of the *Algemeen Handelsblad* of Amsterdam. I'm sorry, I have no cards with me."

He was shown into a small room furnished like an office or a study; it had a large desk in the middle, some bookshelves, a cabinet against the walls, and one or two good pictures. The man sitting behind the desk was younger than Hambledon had expected him to be; he was a fair-haired and broad-shouldered, with hard light eyes and a mouth like a rattrap. Tommy's private comment was, "Poor old Eisenschmidt!" However, he bowed and said, "Herr Norz? Hambledon."

"Please sit down," said Norz, indicating a chair with the end of his pen and nodding to the servant, who went out, leaving the door half open.

"I hope you will forgive this intrusion," said Tommy, and

repeated with a few well-chosen embroideries the account of himself which he had given to Eisenschmidt. "One may be on holiday but one is still a journalist, Herr Norz. Your car——" and so on. Norz sat quite still with his eyes on his visitor's face, nodding occasionally, and waited patiently until Hambledon, as it were, ran down and stopped. Then at last Norz moved, pushing his chair back a trifle with his hands on the arms.

"You may be a Dutchman," he said, "as to that I cannot say, but of the rest of your story I do not believe one word."

Hambledon sat up indignantly, but Norz swept on.

"Whoever heard of a press man without his press card? A genuine one would as soon come out without his clothes. Now I will tell you something about yourself. You travelled from Basle yesterday with a man——"

"I did not, I was travelling alone."

Norz waved him down. "I misled you. I did not mean that you travelled in company, merely that you were on the same train. At Innsbruck he spoke to you, offering to drive you to Seefeld, and you accepted, so he came here to borrow my car. I gather that you guessed it had not been stolen. I went with him to the station; I wanted to have a look at you. You and he drove off; half an hour later he and the car went over a precipice. I suppose you knocked him out and then let the car run off the road. Now, Herr—or Mynheer Hambledon, is it? you will realize that I know what I'm talking about when I ask you; Where are the papers?"

"You may know what you are talking about, but I certainly do not."

Norz assumed an air of enforced patience.

"I will make myself unmistakeably clear. I refer to the papers which a man named Bastien gave you. You remember him?"

"I remember the Herr Bastien very well, but he did not give me any papers. Not even a copy of the *Algemeen Handelsblad.*"

"He died, if you remember," said Norz ominously.

"We all shall when our time comes," said Hambledon cheerfully. "In the meantime, am I right in supposing that my eccentric taxi driver last night was a friend of yours? Do you know, when he told me to undress I thought he was recruiting for a nudist colony? I said so at the time."

Norz sighed and touched a bell on his desk; instantly the servant appeared in the doorway. Hambledon glanced over his shoulder; when he looked back Norz had him covered with an automatic pistol.

"Search him, Hugo."

Since Tommy had nothing on him which could interest them, not even his passport, he made no objection and even stood up to make Hugo's task easier. Everything which was in his pockets was taken out and laid on the desk; his coat was removed and examined and expert hands ran over his body.

"Nothing here," said Hugo.

"Put your coat on again," said Norz. "And put the things back in your pockets."

Hambledon took up his coat, looked at it disdainfully, and brushed with his handkerchief some of the places where Hugo had touched it.

"I would ask you," he said as he slipped his arms into the sleeves, "to lend me a clothesbrush, but I don't expect you have such a thing." He picked up his various trifles from the desk and began to put them back in his pockets. "Nothing here with which I can tempt you? This cigarette case is quite a nice one, isn't it? Of course it isn't an antique, but one can't expect it of a cigarette case, can one ? Do you mind if I smoke?"

Without waiting for an answer he lit a cigarette, put lighter and case into his pocket, sat down again and beamed upon Norz.

"Those papers," began Norz——

"You are a man of one idea, aren't you?" said Tommy admiringly. "Pertinacious, in fact. That isn't a rude word," he added hastily, "in case you don't know it. It means a man who——"

"Stop that!" said Norz sharply. "Those papers are, no doubt, in your language and now you are going to tell me exactly where they are."

"Why?"

"Where are they?"

"I don't know," said Hambledon. "I do know, of course, since we are being all boys together over this matter, that Bastien had some papers somebody else wanted, but he did not give them to me. I have not got them and I have never had them. I don't want them and I am not even remotely interested in them.

Why you are insisting in what I must describe as this rude manner I cannot imagine. I don't even know what the papers, if there really were any to start with, are all about and, to be frank with you, I don't care. I assume that Bastien was supposed to have them with him on that train journey, but how do you know he didn't get rid of them? Burn them or tear them into small pieces and dispose of them in a place so obviously made for the purpose that I can safely leave it to your imagination. Suppose he thought them too hot to handle and lost his nerve?"

"I don't believe it. Papers of that value——"

"You don't want to believe it, you mean. Of course, if you were on to something so big that the proceeds might be expected to keep you and all your loving relations in comfort for the rest of your lives and those of three generations to come, I can understand your disappointment. More, I sympathize. It must be like holding the winning ticket in a really big——"

Norz hammered the desk with the butt of his gun.

"Careful," said Hambledon sharply, "that thing might go off. A really big lottery and then finding you've lost the ticket. I am quite sorry for you, I am really, but I can't help you." He rose to his feet. "Well now, I've quite enjoyed our talk but time is getting on and——"

"You are quite right," said Norz. "Time is getting on, as you said, and yours is nearly up. I cannot imagine what you thought you would gain by all this ridiculous babble——"

"The milkman, of course."

"Milkman?"

"Or the postman or the laundry. Surely you have your sheets washed occasionally? I cannot believe that you make a habit of bumping people off while the bright lad from the local——"

"I wish to be fair," said Norz impressively, and Hambledon was so surprised that his eyebrows shot up. "The evidence that these papers are among your luggage is not, indeed, entirely conclusive, but I fear it will not help you. If you had been prepared to hand them over I would have spared your life because once you had done so, you could not afford to talk. But you have seen fit to refuse. Not only that, but you made your own way here—I did not invite you—and now you have seen us, so I fear that you must die. Hugo!"

Hambledon turned like a flash, his chair broke over Hugo's head and the ruins went through the glass-fronted cabinet. The next moment the table went over——

Herr Lucius Lombard, having had a short interview with his friends, went with one of them to Innsbruck station to see Hambledon arrive. They were not themselves in open view, but Lombard was able to point out to the man with him the spare broad-shouldered figure in grey. The man nodded and strolled after Hambledon while Lombard, keeping well back, strolled after the man who presently came back and said, "He has gone into Eisenschmidt's, the antique shop."

"He has, has he? I think we'll wait."

They waited for twenty minutes.

"He's had time to buy out the shop," said Lombard. "Go along and see if he's still there, will you?"

The man nodded and went along to stare into the shopwindow for a time and then return.

"I don't think there's anyone in the shop," he said. "The old fellow is pottering round with a duster."

"Is there another way out?"

"Only into the yard at the back, mein Herr, and even then you would have to come out this way, by that alley."

Lombard hesitated. "I'll give him another five minutes and then I'll go in myself. I wish I knew who he is and what the devil he's up to."

Lombard waited and then walked along to the shop. He looked in at the window and saw Eisenschmidt tilting up a chair to dust its legs. There seemed to be no one else there. Lombard opened the door and entered. He went straight to the point by saying that he had arranged to meet a friend there but had been delayed and probably missed him. Had his friend, in fact, been in the shop that morning? He described Hambledon and the old man nodded.

"A journalist from Amsterdam? Oh yes. He talked with me

for a time about the car which was stolen and then he went upstairs to talk to the Herr Norz to whom it really belongs!"

"Is he still there, do you know?"

"I have not seen him go, mein Herr, but he may have gone by the private door in the alley; if he did not thereafter pass this window I should not see him."

Lombard did not say that Hambledon had not come from the alley.

"Would the Herr," suggested Eisenschmidt, "like me to ring up the flat and ask if his friend is still there? There is a house telephone, you understand, by which one speaks."

"I think," began Lombard, but was interrupted by a heavy thud overhead and sounds as of furniture being moved.

"That manservant up there," said the old man contemptuously, "is as clumsy as a bull and nearly as strong. He is always making noises."

"I think I won't trouble; my friend must have gone," said Lombard, and left the shop. The moment he was out of sight he broke into a run and his companion came to meet him.

"Go and keep a watch on that place," he said. "I think they have captured our man and they may want to get rid of him quickly. I am going to telephone and then bring my car up a little nearer."

Lombard came back ten minutes later, driving his own car, and was about to stop short of the antique shop when a small open truck came out of the alley and turned to go away from him. He drove on, therefore, and his man, who had been idling in the entrance to a bookshop opposite, came across the road and stepped into the car as Lombard slowed and at once went on again.

"There is a carpet in that truck," the man said. "It does not appear to be tightly rolled and yet it is heavy and stiff." He added the number of the truck.

"Yes," said Lombard. "I shall follow them till they are out of town, but I daren't sit on their tails after that; they would spot me at once. Get your people on the job will you? I think we are going towards the river," he added, and turned right following the truck.

"Drop me off here, please," said the man, and swung himself out as the car slowed.

Polizedirektion, Innsbruck, calling all patrol cars. Look out for small open truck number so-and-so; report place and direction of travel; do not stop it. Polizeidirektion *ringing all police posts; look out for small open truck number so-and-so; report place and direction——*

The truck carried on, not hurrying and sometimes held up by traffic, until it crossed the Inn by the University bridge. Lombard drove decorously behind it until it had turned left up the Inn valley; then he drew out to pass it as a faster car would naturally do, drove ahead of it for a sufficient distance, and then stopped at the entrance to a factory. He got out as the truck passed, saw the two men in it glance indifferently at him, and waited till they were round a bend before he got in again and drove on. He had not gone far before a car came up from behind, just touched its horn in passing, and took the lead. Lombard relaxed a little; this one had been a police car.

As soon as it became known which way the truck was heading, there were watchful eyes along the road, especially at points where side roads turned off. The hunters were fortunate in the road which the truck had taken; since this road lies between the Inn on one hand and the precipitous mountain wall of the valley on the other, there are very few side turnings and most of them are short. There was the crossroads at Zirl, but here a constable, waiting for them on the bridge, waved the police car on and Lombard followed after. They were travelling more slowly now, not wishing to overtake the truck which was pounding along half a mile ahead.

Knauer, Aigenhofen, Dirschenbach, Leiblfing——

"This fellow is making for Switzerland," said the police driver to his assistant.

"Then we'll get him at the frontier," said the other.

At the next village, Unter Pettnau, there was a constable standing where the road forks and he did not wave them on.

"You have not seen it?"

"No," said the constable.

Lombard pulled in behind the police car and there was a conference.

"He's turned off somewhere between here and Leiblfing," said the police driver. "There are a couple of roads, so to call them, going down towards the river."

"I saw them," said Lombard.

"They go into that wood," said the driver.

"So do I," said Lombard. He got back into his car and turned it to face the way they had come.

"What would you like us to do now?"

"Will you stay on the road by the wood? I hope to flush those birds and perhaps they'll fly back to their nests. Wherever they may be, I should like to know where they are." He began to move off and the driver walked beside the car with his hand on the window.

"Will you be all right? Two armed men——"

Lombard grinned at him.

"At least," said the policeman, trotting alongside, "take my whistle." He tossed it into Lombard's lap as the car gathered speed.

Lombard turned into the first road he came to which led across a rough meadow to the woods by the riverside; the car rolled and pitched as far as the trees, where it stopped and Lombard got out. He leaned over the back of his seat, removed a raincoat which had been thrown on the floor, and took up the rifle which the coat had concealed. He loaded it, put some spare cartridges in his pocket, looked at the safety catch to make sure that it was on, and moved forward quietly into the trees.

Ten minutes later he was lying on an outcrop of rock looking down between tree-stems at a small patch of grass which over-hung the river. It had a carpet spread out on it; one man was lying full-length on the carpet and two more were bending over him. They appeared to be cutting and pulling away some rope bonds which were round him. The recumbent man seemed to be unconscious, for he made no effort to resist when he was rolled about. When they had finished, one of the men tidily picked up the pieces of rope and laid them aside.

"Had we better give him some more?" he asked.

"On the contrary," said the other. "I want him to revive a little before he goes in. He must be breathing properly or he won't be drowned, you know; just in case somebody picks the body out later on."

"Nobody won't," said the other, "not out of this torrent. He's going behind the Iron Curtain down the beautiful blue Danube, and they won't worry."

The recumbent figure stirred, threw out one arm, and tried to roll over. The two men watched him; one of them nodded and they stooped over him.

Lombard cuddled his rifle to his shoulder, took careful aim, and fired.

CHAPTER VII

Lucius Lombard

As usually happens when one comes out from unconsciousness, Hambledon had been able to hear distinctly and understand some time before he could move, even open his eyes. He heard the steady rush of the river and the calm plans being made to throw him in it, and he was quite well aware that in that bitter cold water with its twisting currents even a thoroughly fit swimmer stands very little chance, for the Inn is even more deadly than the Rhine. He determined to lie perfectly still until his strength came back; then, when they bent over him——

But his limbs would not obey him; it seemed as though even as they regained consciousness they stirred of their own accord; he could not prevent it. He would draw his legs up and hope that he could still kick. Even as he did so, there came a crack which he recognized as that of a rifle near by, and another and yet another. He opened his eyes and saw Norz standing over him with an automatic in his hand, but it had not been fired; it was not that—even as Norz raised it there was another crack and something peculiar happened to Norz's wrist. He uttered a yell of pain and dropped the automatic on Hambledon's legs. The next moment there was the sound of running feet; when he turned his head there was no one to be seen. He tried to sit up but the effort made his head swim and he collapsed again.

He came round a few minutes later with the feeling that there was someone near him; this time he would not give himself away.

"The Herr," said a pleasant voice which sounded familiar, "likes to sun-bathe in luxury, evidently."

Hambledon opened his eyes and looked round; a pair of very sturdy legs in woollen stockings first presented themselves. His eyes travelled upwards to wide grey suede knickers, a sports jacket, and finally the cheerful moon-face of Herr Lombard beaming down on him. Lombard had a rifle in one hand with the butt resting on the ground.

"The carpet," went on Lombard, "looks a particularly good one, to me." He bent down, took up one corner of the carpet, and examined the back. "Genuine Persian. Dear me. A little blood-stained in one place, but that can be easily removed."

Fresh air and sunshine were clearing Hambledon's head quickly. He sat up and said sharply, "Who the devil are you?"

"Lucius Lombard, of the Austrian Special Police, at your service."

"Last night you told me you were a traveller in mouth organs from Munich. May I see your official card?"

Lombard's face creased into a comic picture of rueful embarrassment as he felt in his jacket pockets. Hambledon sat upright and became aware that he was sitting on something hard; he put his hand down, the hard thing was Norz's automatic. He kept it in his hand under his coat.

"I am so sorry," said Lombard. "When I changed into this sporting kit this morning I did not transfer the card from my other coat pocket. Why should I? The chamois, you know, would not ask for it."

"But I'm no chamois," said Hambledon, and the automatic in his hand flashed up and was levelled at Lombard. "Drop that gun and put your hands up!"

Lombard obeyed at once; the rifle fell to the ground. The hand which had been in his pocket went up with the other, accompanied by a gleam of silver which travelled no further than his mouth, and immediately there came the ear-piercing blast of a police whistle energetically blown. Hambledon, taken by surprise, yet pulled the rifle towards him in order to throw it into the river.

"Don't do that," said Lombard, sibilantly, round the whistle; "it'sh a good gun. Shh!"

There came the sound of heavy boots violently running, and two uniformed policemen burst through the bushes with revolvers in their hands.

"Thank you," said Lombard, letting fall the whistle. "Please tell this gentleman who I am. He may believe you."

They said in firm official voices that that was in fact the Herr Lombard, a highly placed officer in the Austrian Special Police.

"You may put your hands down," said Hambledon in a resigned voice, and laid down the automatic. Lombard told the two policemen to take it and his rifle and retire out of earshot but not out of sight. "This gentleman and I have a few words to exchange and I think he may talk more freely in private. Keep your eyes open all round; we do not wish to be the subject of target practice by those carpet merchants."

"They are gone, mein Herr. They got into the car and moved off. We were in the act of starting after them when your whistle blew."

"Your whistle, you mean," said Lombard, returning it to the driver. "Well, that's a pity but it can't be helped. Thank you."

The police retired and Lombard lowered himself slowly onto the carpet, being careful to avoid the bloodstains.

"Excuse me, may I occupy a corner of your priceless Shiraz? Thank you. First of all, do you believe now that I am a policeman?"

"Certainly," said Hambledon. "I should apologize for doubting you, but you will admit that some of your statements were rather equivocal; besides, there was the rifle. Now, I suppose, it's your turn to bend over me and murmur, 'Tell me, where are those papers?'"

"I should, indeed, like to know that, but I think I will start by asking you who you are."

"I am Thomas Elphinstone Hambledon, British subject, resident in London and at the moment on holiday in the Austrian Tyrol."

"Thank you. Now, if you are merely on holiday, how did you come to be connected with all this business about the papers?"

"That was just sheer bad luck. I happened to be sharing a sleeping compartment, on the Anglo-Swiss Express to Basle, with a man who was shot." Hambledon told the story in full detail. "So now the French police are hunting for the man called Pierre and I hope they find him. As for the papers he was demanding, I haven't got them, I never saw them, and Bastien never said a word to me about them. Why should he? A total stranger."

"I see. Well now, Herr Hambledon, I am going to put all my cards on the table for you to see. If you are, so to speak, on our side I think it will do no harm; if you are on the other side I will see that it does not! Now, then.

"There is an organization here in Europe which makes a speciality of really large operations. They would not stoop to burgle the ordinary small private house, but if a consignment of gold bars is missing in transit by air——" He paused. "Perhaps you remember? Or if some man in an important position, especially with access to public funds, is blackmailed——"

"And perhaps commits suicide," said Hambledon.

"Oh, that was one of their failures. They have had their successes. Those papers of which you speak were stolen; good money would be paid for them either to get them back or to acquire them. Eh? The point I am trying to make is that they are not interested in little things; their business deals run into thousands. When it is stolen jewellery it is not the diamond brooch of the mayor's wife; it is jewels which have adorned a Queen." He paused again and Hambledon nodded.

"Well now, of course InterPol is after them and has been for years and I, in my small way, am taking a hand. There have been certain indications that the centre of the web is somewhere in this area, in West Tyrol. I myself would circumscribe the area more closely; I think it is somewhere in the Seefeld-Mittenwald district."

"Across a frontier."

"Yes. They might find that helpful. I have been hanging round this district for more than three months now trying to find the spot—and the man."

"And, incidentally, selling mouth organs?"

"Even so," said Lombard without a smile.

"I beg your pardon, then." said Hambledon. "Please go on."

"When I was informed about these stolen papers I naturally wondered whether they might come this way, so I spent the whole of yesterday at Innsbruck station watching the arrival of trains from Basle to see if anyone interesting came on any of them. Not until the twenty-one thirty train last night was my patience rewarded when a man named Dublè walked out of the station." Lombard stopped and cocked an eyebrow at Hambledon, but he merely looked blank and shook his head.

"You walked out with him, Herr Hambledon, chatting amicably and on the best of terms, and one of the outside porters told me that you arranged to meet him there again in an hour's time; the label on your rucksack in the left-luggage office told me you were going to Seefeld."

"I see," said Hambledon, taking out his cigarette case. "Will you smoke?"

"Thank you," said Lombard, taking one. "I like English cigarettes. To return to last night, you went to the Hochhaus and I hope you enjoyed your meal, while Dublè went to the antique shop and borrowed Norz's Citroën. All went according to plan. When you and Dublè drove away from Innsbruck station I came along too at a tactful distance. There was no need to sit on your tail because, you see, I knew where you were going. Besides, where else would you go, on that road? I must say I was very surprised when I saw from a distance—and heard—that spectacular crash when the car went over the edge. I thought you were both killed and I was genuinely grieved. Imagine, therefore, my astonishment when, a little later on, I recognized you sitting at the side of the road hoping for a lift. May I say, too, how much I admired your bit of byplay with the shoe off and the sock being gently eased over the painful heel? I was really touched by the pathetic little story you told about having spent the whole day hiking from Innsbruck."

Hambledon laughed.

"Coming to this morning, the first thing you do is to announce your intention of going to Innsbruck, so naturally I got there first in order to have a little parley with the Chief of Police at *Polizeidirektion.* He lent me a plain-clothes man to whom I pointed you out when you left the station. He followed you, naturally, and where did you go? As a bee to its hive, Herr Hambledon, as a bird to its nest, straight to poor old Eisenschmidt's antique shop. Not only that. When, after a decent lapse of time, I went into the shop to see if you were still there, the old boy told me you had gone upstairs to see Herr Norz, you being a journalist from Amsterdam."

Lombard pitched his cigarette end into the river, drew up his knees, and clasped his hands round them.

"What did you think," said Hambledon, "when you saw those two charming young men preparing to murder me this morning?"

"Either that you were not one of the gang and had found out a little too much, or that they were merely taking reprisals because you had deprived them of Dublè. In either case I proposed to rescue you; if you are innocent you deserve it and if you are guilty you may be able to tell me something. Perhaps quite a lot. Now, Herr Hambledon, no doubt you will see the advisability of laying your cards on the table in your turn. I have been frank with you; be frank with me and don't pull this innocent-tourist-on-holiday stuff over my eyes. Who are you and what were you doing in that galley?"

"In the first place, I am Hambledon of British Intelligence, but it is also true that I am here for a holiday."

"But you have, no doubt, your official card?"

"Not with me," said Hambledon firmly; "it's in my room at the hotel." At Lombard's look he broke into a laugh. "Damn it, man, you couldn't produce yours."

"But I could and did produce a couple of policemen to vouch for me. Can you?"

"Not in Austria. However, that's where it is and I'll show it to you presently. Now for my story. I told you all about poor Bastien being shot in my compartment. When the police came they were headed by a Detective Inspector named Virolet and I showed him my card." Hambledon told Lombard the whole story in detail, including the visit to Bastien's flat and the conversation on the tape recorder. "Cournand of the Basle police took us to the café and we got some more information there with descriptions of those three men."

"I'll ask for them," said Lombard.

Hambledon told him about being offered a lift to Seefeld. "The man didn't tell me his name; that's why I looked so blank when you mentioned Dublè." He went on with an account of the run and being held up by Dublè; the amused Lombard shook like a jelly. "I may as well admit that I had my doubts about you," said Hambledon, "especially when you turned up at the Karwendelhof just as I was going up to bed. You hadn't said you were staying in Seefeld and I was in a doubting mood by then."

"I wasn't going to, until I met you. Then I thought I would stay the night and see what you were up to."

"Yes. One thing you said just now puzzled me. You said you were genuinely grieved when Dublè went down and it sounded as though you meant it."

"I did. I don't want the small fry to die. I want them to lead me on to higher things. I could have shot those two here this morning quite comfortably but I didn't wish to. I only fired over their heads to frighten them away so that if they run, I may run after them and see where they go. It wasn't till Norz produced his gun that I hit him in the arm. Well, shall we go? My stomach says it's lunch time and so, I daresay, does yours."

"That is quite true, it does," said Hambledon. He was an active man, but he noticed that Lombard was on his feet as soon as he. "Shall we take the carpet?"

"One of the police can carry it easily since you are no longer inside it," said Lombard, and gave the order. They walked back towards the cars and Lombard picked up his rifle in passing.

"You prefer that," said Hambledon, "to a pistol? It is not so easily portable and a lot more conspicuous."

"I do prefer it," said Lombard with emphasis. "You may have noticed that nature has made me a rather large target. Yes. Imagine me trying to walk up within pistol range of some skinny little man who can cover himself completely behind a birch tree. With this I can lie off and exterminate my enemies at long range."

"Are you going back to Seefeld now," asked Hambledon, "or will you drop me off where I can get a bus or something?"

"Herr Hambledon," said Lombard reproachfully, "after a whole two hours spent in contemplation of my sparkling intelligence! What do you take me for? You are coming to the *Polizeidirektion* at Innsbruck, of course."

Hambledon hesitated and the police closed up.

"Oh, come on," said Lombard, "be reasonable. They will give you lunch there and I'll see it's a good one. It is only till I can get on to the Seefeld police to go and look in your room for your card and then ring up and tell me they've found it. Put yourself in my place. What would——"

Hambledon laughed and gave in. The two cars drove back to Innsbruck in company, but Hambledon travelled in the back seat of the police car with a watchful policeman sitting beside him. The Central Police Station at Innsbruck is in the Sillgasse, just off Universitatsstrasse; when the car actually drove in there the Englishman heaved a small sigh of relief. After all, police uniforms have been known to be stolen.

Lombard excused himself for a moment and went away to telephone to Seefeld, or so he said; ten minutes later he came back with a man, elderly but very smart and upright, whom he introduced as Herr Pfeffer, the Chief of Police, and it was at once evident to Tommy that the Chief had a divided mind. If his visitor were really Hambledon of British Intelligence he should be heartily welcomed and suitably entertained; if he were an imposter, handcuffs and a cell should be his portion. Herr Pfeffer, like a man on a tightrope, maintained an expert balance between the two extremes; he bowed; he did not shake hands, nor did he sit down.

"The Herr Hambledon? I have heard of you and it will be an honour to me to associate with such a man. I have telephoned to my fellows at Seefeld and I expect the answer very shortly. In the meantime, it is past our lunch hour, but I understand that neither you nor Herr Lombard has lunched yet. I propose that we send out for something. Herr Lombard, you suggest——"

"Shall I deal with it?" asked Lombard. "If I may use your phone——"

He was in the middle of discussing a menu with The Grey Bear when a clerk came in to call the Chief of Police to the telephone; when he returned he was smiling.

"Herr Hambledon, as soon as my man reached the Karwendelhof and stated his errand, the management asked if he could get in touch with you. There have been two telephone calls from London for you this morning; the second asked that you would please ring up a certain number at the earliest possible moment as it is urgent. I have noted down the number. Here it is."

Hambledon looked at it.

"I expect this is important; it is the number of my Department of the Foreign Office. If I might——"

"Will you use the telephone in my room? I will get you a priority call, it will be quicker," said the Chief, and strode out of the room. Lombard hung up his telephone and Hambledon asked if he had heard what had been said. "It may be this same job," he added. "I hope it is."

"I hope so, too," said Lombard. "It might be quite amusing if we two worked together."

"I think so, indeed, and though I expect my holiday won't be the quiet relaxation I hoped for, at least my Government will now pay my expenses—I trust."

"Work or play," said Lombard sententiously, "there will be the same magnificent fresh air to expand the lungs, vitalize the blood, and invigorate the system."

"Are you practicing a good line of talk for a travel agency?"

"I am always practicing something," said Lombard.

The Chief of Police came back and said the London call was through.

"My goodness," said Tommy, getting up hastily, "they have been quick."

"It is my doing," said the Chief, leading the way. "I terrorized them." He shut Hambledon in alone with the telephone and came back.

"It looks as though he is really genuine," he said. "Don't you agree?"

"I should be very pleased to do so," said Lombard cautiously. "I like him and he is no fool."

"Far from it," said the Chief. "If he is really that Hambledon, he is a very distinguished man indeed. Even I have heard of him."

"We shall hear soon from Seefeld," said Lombard in a low tone.

"But," said the Chief, rather scandalized, "are you proposing to hold a man like that——"

"Don't worry, there will be no difficulty about that. He wants his lunch, remember, and so do I. We will have it here, and long before we have done we shall hear from Seefeld."

The door opened and Hambledon returned.

"They are holding the line," he said to the Chief of Police. "They would like to speak to you."

Pfeffer went out and Hambledon sat down.

"It was that," he said. "They want those papers back or else."

"Henceforth," said Lombard magnificently, "we are brothers-in-arms."

"Putting myself in your place," began Hambledon——

"Well?"

"I should want to hear from Seefeld."

"You have a nasty suspicious mind," said Lucius Lombard.

CHAPTER VIII

Two Cinzanos

The Chief of Police came back into the room with a light step and a confident expression.

"You are to have all the assistance you may need," he said, "and may I say how delighted I shall be to supply it? I hope you will regard our resources as being at all times entirely at your disposal. Indeed, Herr Hambledon, I regard this as an honour."

"Thank you very much," said Tommy. "Of course, you will get a written confirmation of all this by air mail. It is very good of you to promise your help at once."

"They are very slow with that lunch," said Pfeffer, fidgeting, but there came a knock at the door and heavy trays were carried in. "I will leave you for a time, if you will excuse me. I have a few odds and ends to tidy up." He went away. When the meal had been set out Lombard and Hambledon were left alone and there was an interval of busy silence.

"Tell me," said Lombard eventually, "do your people agree with me that the centre of this business is somewhere in this district?"

"They didn't say so. I don't know that they have any very definite views. Why?"

"They put you on to it here, surely? And authorized you to the Austrian police?"

"Ah, but you don't quite understand. From their point of view it's me that's here, not necessarily your big bad man. As for the

Austrian police, they aren't the only ones; there are also police in Germany, Switzerland, and Italy all itching to lend a hand. InterPol, in fact. You know," said Hambledon, laying down his knife and fork, "this looks like being quite a show, doesn't it? Of course, you are rather surrounded by various frontiers here. By the way, naturally you'll be hearing from your own head office at any moment now. Imploring you to assist and comfort me, I mean."

"Of course," said Lombard. "I expect——"

"In the meantime," said Tommy blandly, "Seefeld are taking quite a time, aren't they? This is very excellent beer."

"I should have thought they would answer before this, certainly. I told the man exactly where you said it was."

Tommy laughed and Lombard asked him what the joke was.

"I was only wondering what you would say if my room has been broken into and my card stolen. I mean, you'd be back where you were, wouldn't you, for what is a telephone message? Just a voice."

"I should think——" began Lombard, but was interrupted by the hasty entrance of the Chief of Police.

"Seefeld," he said. "The hotel is in a state of suppressed upset, if I may so put it. 'What a dreadful thing! Do something but don't say anything; we must not alarm the customers.'" He laughed. "All the same, it is very odd. They sent one man up there authorized to enter your room and, as he knows the hotel perfectly well, they just gave him the key and didn't send anybody up with him. He was some time but nobody worried; they did not know how long he expected to be. Then the housemaid in charge of that floor rang down and said that when she was passing Herr Hambledon's door she heard groans——"

"Don't tell me," said Hambledon in a hollow voice, "that I'm turning into a prophet? Not a true prophet, please."

"And the housemaid couldn't get the door open because it was locked from inside and the key in the lock, and she was frightened. She didn't know there was a policeman in there; she thought it was Herr Hambledon taken ill and would somebody do something? So the management, who were better informed, rang up the police again and another man came up and broke in the door. The first policeman was lying on the floor groaning, with a lump on the top of his head, and everything in the room was thrown all over the place. Your rucksack, Herr Hambledon, was slit to ribbons."

"I can't bear the suspense," said Tommy. "Before anything else, did your policeman find my card?"

"Oh yes. He read it out to me; that's all right."

Lombard laughed aloud.

"They seem to think," went on the Chief of Police, "that a man slipped up the stairs, picked the lock, and went in. Not long after, the first policeman arrived and rattled the key into the lock, which alarmed the man inside. When our man walked in, the other fellow, probably standing behind the door, hit him hard on the head with something and knocked him out, locked the door leaving the key in the lock, and went on searching. Presently our man started to groan and the housemaid heard him, so she knocked on the door and called through it. The intruder realized his time was up and left by sliding down the supports of the balcony. You could, you know. I have stayed at the Karwendelhof myself and I have a phobia about fire. You could not climb up those balconies but an active man could get down. I mean, he must have done so, because when the door was broken in he was not there."

"Is the policeman hurt?" asked Hambledon.

"They said only concussion and he is already better, but he cannot remember anything, not even opening the door. They would like you to return and check your things in case there is anything missing."

"I don't expect there is," said Tommy. "I can't think of anything there they'd want except a brand-new electric razor. You know, Lombard, when Norz went through me after they doped me this morning and didn't find what they were looking for, he must have telephoned to somebody."

"Who lives at or near Seefeld," said Lombard.

"Yes. Well, now where are we? Since he didn't find——"

"Just a moment. Are you perfectly sure that the late Herr Bastien did not plant the papers on you while you were asleep? It's a very old trick, to induce someone who is both innocent and ignorant to carry something for one, and, of course, you were quite unsuspecting."

"I have thought of that and I don't see where he could have put them. In fact, I've looked. I had only my rucksack with not much in it—things for the night—and my clothes hanging up on a peg. No, he didn't do that."

"Is one rucksack all the luggage you had?"

"No," said Hambledon, "and that reminds me, I have not collected them yet. I have two suitcases in the customs shed at Seefeld; at least, I hope they are there. But Bastien could not possibly have put anything in them because I registered them through from London to Seefeld direct. I never saw them myself after I parted with them in London."

"No, I see," said Lombard thoughtfully, "but will your pursuers know that?"

Hambledon considered. "The man who went over the precipice, Dublè? Yes, Dublè—he was presumably watching me from the moment I got off the train at Innsbruck——"

"It doesn't matter," said Lombard. "If you are openly seen and heard to be demanding the rest of your luggage from the customs shed at Seefeld, they won't trouble about how it travelled. It will be your luggage and that will be enough. Then you will take out your baggage and carry it over to the hotel. In the meantime I shall be hanging about to see if anyone takes any interest in you. You, most esteemed Herr Hambledon, are going to be the cheese in the mousetrap."

"Yes, I thought you had some such idea. Where are you going to be?"

"Oh, I shall stay at the Karwendelhof too. I will ask for a room along your corridor, but I don't think we'd better be seen much together."

"No. I was going to suggest your giving me a lift up to Seefeld by road, but perhaps I'd better travel separately, by train. By the way, those two this morning, Norz and—what was the other thug's name? Hugo, that's it—did they see you among the trees pooping off at them, you know?"

"I asked the police that. The answer is no. They fled, pausing only to tie up Norz's wrist. What is more, they did not go home to the antique shop in the Lieberstrasse, at least, not straight home. Of course, they may do so later. The police didn't chase them if you remember——"

"But surely," said Hambledon, "they must know I should complain to the police?"

"But surely," echoed Lombard, "that all depends who and what you are? If you're running round Europe with stolen designs for guided missiles, you wouldn't cling round the police much, would you?"

"You may be right but if I were they, I wouldn't go home. That reminds me. My department told me about somebody else who hasn't gone home—that Russian fellow who was buying the said designs from a Frenchman in the back room of a café in Basle. He left Basle but apparently did not return to Berne, and my department says that the Swiss police think he was heading this way, but he does not seem to have crossed any frontiers."

"We have, in Tyrol, tourists from many nations," said Lombard, "but very seldom are they Russian. Do you know anything about him? His personal appearance? Is he a good linguist and so on?"

"Details to follow by post."

"As for crossing frontiers——"

"Oh, quite," said Tommy Hambledon.

When a train is expected, Seefeld station is a scene of leisurely activity; there are the people going, the people seeing them off, and the people waiting to greet arrivals. Conspicuous among these are the representatives of the various travel agencies in labelled hats or badged blazers and also porters from the different hotels waiting for their prey. The customs men stand about in a group, talking confidentially together, and an Austrian State Railways porter or two may wheel a loaded truck slowly beside the railway line. Nobody rushes about or gets excited or catches a train at the last second, for such is not the Tyrolese way of life. The flowering meadows, in June as many-coloured as a bright carpet, break in a spray of blossom against the railway fence; beyond the meadows the dark green pines cloak the lower slopes of the mountains; above the pines moss and bare rock climb halfway up the sky to be ultimately crested with snow, bright silver against the blue. As a rule the sun shines and the air is such that any man who does not find himself unreasonably exhilarated should instantly consult a doctor.

However, when Hambledon strolled across to the station from the Karwendelhof at about ten on the following morning, no train was expected and there were very few people about at all. There were some of the hotel guests half asleep in deck chairs in the sun on the Karwendelhof's little strip of lawn; there were some of the hotel servants scurrying about with bursts of laughter upon unguessable errands; there was an elderly woman mowing, with a scythe, the lawns of some gardens opposite; and there was a long, thin, gangling figure of a man leaning on the iron railings watching her. He turned his head when he heard the gritty crunch of Hambledon's shoes on the road. The head was crowned with a completely shapeless felt hat which may have been green to start with but was certainly so with age; stuck upright at the back of the hat was a slim wavering feather a foot long with a broken tip.

Hambledon glanced at him and walked on across the station yard. The main entrance door was shut, so he retraced his steps past the little tobacco-shop inset in the corner of the station buildings and made his way onto the platform. The wind stirred in the trees and blew cool against his cheek. There came the distant sound of cow bells and the nearer sound of children's voices in the wood, the rattle of a loose chain tapping just below the notice which says *"Wasser nicht für trinken,"* and nothing else.

Tommy Hambledon strolled the whole length of the station, past the customs shed and back again; whenever he came to a door he knocked upon it but nobody opened to him. He was standing near the booking office looking across the railway lines at a white-walled cottage in the meadow opposite; it stood alone and there was a coloured fresco of a man, more than life-size, upon the wall facing him. Hambledon was studying it with interest when he became aware rather than heard that there was someone near him. He turned sharply. It was the man with the tall feather in his hat.

Hambledon said *"Grüss Gott,"* the pleasant greeting which is always used in those parts, and the man answered *"Grüss Gott"* with a grin which showed that he had only two teeth in his top jaw and even they were not near neighbours.

"That picture," said Tommy, pointing it out.

"Yes," nodded the man, "picture," and his tall feather waggled idiotically.

"It is a railway man," said Hambledon.

"Yes. Railway man."

"Why?" asked Tommy.

The man looked up at the hilltop for inspiration and apparently got it. "He lives there."

"Who lives there?"

"Railway man."

"Gosh," said Tommy to himself, "I've got the village idiot." The man grinned again and moved off a little to stare vacantly up and down the line. Hambledon looked at him. He had a thin face with a beaky nose and a long scrawny neck with a prominent Adam's apple. His clothes, which were old and worn, had once belonged to someone smaller than he, for the legs of his trousers did not reach his socks nor the sleeves of his jackets, his wrists. On one wrist was a form of wrist watch which must, Hambledon thought, have been one of the first ever made, for it consisted of a strap more than an inch wide bearing a clumsy case to hold an ordinary pocket watch and a cheap one at that. The man's hair was unkempt and so long that it fell in elflocks on his collar; his face was, by contrast, neatly and cleanly shaven.

He must have felt Hambledon's eyes upon him, for he turned with a foolish grin and said, "The Herr desires——?"

"People here," said Hambledon, with a wave of the hand towards the station buildings and suiting his conversation to his company. "Nobody at home?"

"Not now. Presently. At a quarter before eleven." The man glanced up at the sun and then, as though suddenly remembering that he had a watch, he looked down at his wrist instead.

"The Herr comes again, yes?"

"Thank you," said Tommy, tiring of his company. "I will come back presently." He nodded to the man but had no acknowledgement; it seemed that the watch needed winding.

There is a train to Innsbruck at a quarter to eleven. Hambledon waited till it had gone and then went to the customs shed. The officers were lenient with him, a few formal questions and they chalked his cases. He walked along to the gate, carrying them; the moment he was outside the man with the feather was there, at his elbow.

"To carry the Herr's bags, please?"

"Don't bother, thank you," said Tommy, fending him off. "It's not worth it, only just across to the Karwen——"

"The Herr must not fatigue himself," said the man. "Please." He twitched the suitcases from Hambledon's fingers and shambled ahead; his legs had somehow the air of having been insecurely attached to him but he made nothing of the burden. When they came to the porch he set the cases down, and Tommy gave him a couple of Austrian schillings for his trouble. The man whipped off his hat with a spacious gesture. For a moment Hambledon had the absurd impression that he was about to burst into song, but he only grinned amiably and wandered away.

Hambledon went up to his room to unpack and presently Lombard, having waited until he was not observed, came in also.

"Do sit down," said Hambledon, clearing shirts off a chair. "Did you see anybody taking an interest in me except the village idiot? I didn't, though now I come to think of it, I didn't see you either."

"My eyes were on you," said Lombard solemnly. "They were also on the village idiot, so I went round to the police station to ask about him. They know him, of course; his name is Horaz. Christian name, that is; his surname seems less clear. He comes from our more remote out-back somewhere and moons about doing odd jobs, carrying luggage, shovelling coke, peeling potatoes, and so on. He resides, if you can call it that, in one of those little wooden huts of which you see so many here. He does odd jobs for the farmer who lets him sleep there, though of course he will have to turn out when they want to put the hay in it. Animals like him and he's good with them as simpletons so often are. Sometimes he vanishes for a week or so and turns up again; nobody worries."

"In fact he's just what he looks," said Hambledon. "Pass, Horaz, all's well. By the way, I take it our searcher yesterday didn't find my official card since it is still where I'd put it."

Lombard picked up Hambledon's small travelling clock in its leather case and slipped it out; the card was still tucked away behind it.

"I don't suppose he gave this clock a second glance; it's much too small to conceal what he wanted to find."

Hambledon nodded. "I wonder whether he did find it and, if so, where."

Lombard shrugged his shoulders. "Your welfare, though the subject of my utmost care, will tell us whether he did or not."

Hambledon spent the day strolling about Seefeld talking to people and generally enjoying himself in a mild way. Lombard in his car went past without a greeting, headed for Scharnitz and the German frontier. Perhaps he was going to sell mouth organs in Mittenwald, if such a thing be possible in the town of violins.

There is a cellar beneath the Karwendelhof Hotel. Probably there is more than one but only one is of importance to the guests. It is quite large and is provided with a bar complete with tall stools; numerous small tables and chairs are everywhere except upon a small space of floor, in front of the bar, kept clear for dancing. There is an orchestra consisting of a violinist, a pianist, and a third man who plays percussion instruments and sings. A very wide fireplace is filled with glowing logs if the evening is chilly. One goes to the *Keller* by way of stairs going down behind the entrance hall, and there is also a separate entrance from the outside world by which the young men of Seefeld drop in to drink a glass of wine and see what the tourist agencies have sent them in the way of dancing partners.

Hambledon went down to the *Keller* that evening after dinner and looked about him. Lombard, who, it seemed, had acquired a couple of ladies, was sitting at a table on the far side, near the orchestra. Hambledon recognized several of the hotel guests who had been in the dining room for dinner and one of them, a pleasant elderly man with a grey-haired wife, asked him to sit at their table. It was not their first visit to Seefeld and they talked agreeably about the locality; they were walkers, it appeared. The dance band played at intervals and the floor filled with circling couples; the lighting was soft and the atmosphere pleasant. Hambledon prepared to enjoy himself. A photographer came round from table to table with camera and flash bulb taking photographs of laughing groups. He was so immersed in his business that he did not notice at once that he was being followed round by two of the waiters, one winding the handle of a mincing machine for a camera and the other holding up a round flat tin from the kitchen to simulate the flash-bulb reflector. They crept after the photographer, mimicking every motion, until he looked round to see what was so amusing his customers; then the waiters fled in pretended terror pursued by the photographer in assumed wrath, and all passed from sight.

"Lighthearted people, the Austrians," said Hambledon's friend. "It doesn't seem to weigh on their minds, having been defeated in two world wars. They're always up to some unpremeditated mischief like that, all of a sudden quite without warning; and with squeals of joy everybody joins in."

"They were always like that," said Tommy Hambledon. "I never knew Austria very well, but I do remember Vienna——"

"Ah," said a gay voice behind them. " 'Vienna, city of my dreams!' "

They looked round. A lady sitting at the next table, who appeared to be rather detached from her immediate neighbours, leaned across to them and asked in an arch whisper if she might join their little party. There was, naturally, only one answer possible, and Hambledon got up to turn her chair round for her and received, over her shoulder, a quite blatant wink from the young man of the couple from whom she had just parted. She was a tall gawky Englishwoman in the fifties with a long thin neck and a long thin nose to match.

"Thank you so very much," she said, "so kind." She leaned her elbows on the table and spoke confidentially under cover of "*Du bist die schönste*" from the orchestra. "Those dear young people, just married, you know. They live at Wimbledon, they tell me, and he works in a shipping office in Cockspur Street, so interesting. But this is, I gather, their honeymoon and I did not wish to play gooseberry any longer, if you see what I mean. Two's company, and all that."

"Completely," said Tommy.

"That's the great charm of travel, to my mind," the lady went on. "Meeting so many people and enlarging so interestingly one's circle of acquaintances. May I introduce myself? My name is Wiggins, Agatha Wiggins." She paused and looked expectantly at the grey-haired lady.

"Our name is Grantham," she answered. "This is my husband Colonel Grantham."

"Delighted. And——"

"Hambledon," said Tommy.

"Mr.—ah—Hambledon? Delighted. Well now, do tell me. Does one, as it were, whistle up the photographer or does he just happen along, as the Americans say?"

"He seems to have vanished at the moment." said Colonel Grantham, looking about him. "I daresay that he will return later."

"Very likely. What charming country this is, is it not? So quaint, with all those little huts dotted about. I wonder what they use them for. Surely the peasants do not live in them? For one thing, they have no chimneys, have they, though I suppose one could boil a kettle on a primus stove?"

After a quarter of an hour of this, Mrs. Grantham gathered up her handbag and said that she thought it was bedtime. "But don't you hurry, Arthur, if you are not sleepy."

"But I am," said her husband. "It's the air, you know." They rose and Tommy also managed to make his escape, murmuring something about a man he wanted to speak to. He retired to the bar where he stood himself a Cinzano and, when he had finished that, another.

He exchanged casual comments with his nearest neighbours and was idly listening to an argument about trout fishing when he became aware that the room was uncomfortably hot. It was true that he was near the fire, but the heat did not seem to be troubling anyone else. In fact, as he looked rather dazedly about him he noticed a girl close by who, with a slight shiver, pulled a scarf over her shoulders. They were, actually, very much less effectively covered than Hambledon's, but even so——

It dawned on him that it was he who was hot, not the room and, what was more, it was beginning to swing about.

He slipped from his stool, made his way to the outer door, and struggled up the steps into the fresh air.

CHAPTER IX

Medeski

The air revived Hambledon for a time. He was sitting on the low wall outside breathing deep breaths when he heard a step behind him and looked round to see Lombard at his shoulder.

"Are you all right?"

"No," said Tommy in a puzzled voice, "and I haven't had much this evening. Either I'm losing my grip or the Cinzano they serve here is something especially special." He thought over that that sentence and repeated "special." "I think I'll go to bed." He stood up, staggering, and Lombard took him by the arm.

"I thought you'd turned a rather queer colour," he said. "We'll go this way."

They went along the front of the hotel and in at the main entrance. The hall was almost deserted since most of the guests were in the *Keller* below. This was as well since Hambledon made heavy weather of getting up the stairs.

"Come on," said Lombard, supporting him. "Not much further."

Hambledon lurched against him as they went down the passage in which were both their rooms. "'S a long way tonight."

"That's all right," said Lombard reassuringly. "Nearly there."

In point of fact Hambledon was perfectly right; it was further than usual, for he was being taken to Lombard's room instead of his own, but by the time the door was open he was past noticing a detail like that. He collapsed with a grunt upon the bed and lost consciousness completely.

Lombard hoisted his legs onto the bed, put a pillow under his head, and stood looking at him.

"I suppose you are only doped and not poisoned, or ought I to get a doctor? No, they wouldn't kill you here, far too much fuss." He lifted one of Hambledon's eyelids and looked closely at the pupil. "You'll be all right. Sleep well."

Lombard collected one or two things he thought he might need and then left the room, putting the light out and locking the door after him. He walked quite normally and casually along the passage. If anyone was about he would say he had been up to his room and was now going down again. However, there was no one about; when he had made quite sure of this he went into Hambledon's room, drew the curtains across the windows before he switched on the light and left it on for five minutes by his watch. Someone might conceivably have been watching this window from the public park upon which it looked.

Lombard put a chair at the foot of the bed, behind the door, switched out the light, and sat down to wait.

Hambledon awoke in the morning with a splitting headache and a general sense of undeserved retribution, but Lombard, who knew what to expect and had prepared for it, was ready with the appropriate remedies.

"Thank you," said Tommy, after a reasonable lapse of time. "I feel like a human being again. Now tell me what happened."

"You were doped, of course, and the idea was that you should stagger, or be helped, up to bed where you would then take no notice of whatever happened, and the searchers could go through all your luggage and the clothes you were wearing without being hurried or disturbed." Lombard laughed. "He must have got a shock, poor man."

"You dumped me in here and sat up in my room yourself. I've gathered that much. Well?"

"I sat in a chair at the foot of your bed. I was very anxious that whoever came should not see me clearly and realize that I was not you, so I took out the bulb from the light which turns on from the door. There is a certain amount of light, from street lamps and so forth, which filters in through those thin curtains. By the time I had sat there for half an hour I could see well enough—not details or features, but well enough. He tried the door handle. Of course you would have been too far gone to lock it, so I did not; he came in and shut the door behind him. It must have been very dark to him. Of course, I was standing up before he entered and I went for him like a wildcat. I mean that. I wanted to mark him. Unfortunately it didn't work out quite as I had intended. I got home on one ear and I hope I gave him a black eye, but he recoiled against that little table near the door and his hand, I suppose, encountered that bottle you put there. Why do you bring mineral water up to your bedroom? It is so uncalled for."

"It's a habit," said Hambledon apologetically. "I expect the tap water here is perfectly wholesome, but in most Continental hotels it's asking for trouble to drink it. I always have a bottle of Perrier or something—what did he do with it? Crown you?"

Lombard felt his head tenderly. "I've still got a bump. I didn't pass out at once. I clung to the end of the bed and kicked him on the shin. He opened the door and left me and I staggered over and turned the key. A couple of hours later I woke up, on the carpet against the door, so I don't think he came back. I had a headache so I borrowed your bed for the rest of the night. When we've both had a bath and a shave and a nice breakfast we will go out and look for somebody with a thick ear and a black eye."

"We will go separately," agreed Hambledon, "peering about for bung eyes and cauliflower ears. He must think I'm a pretty tough guy, must he not? Flat out one minute and fighting mad the next. Perhaps it takes some people that way though personally I've never met one. Generally when a man is as flat out as I was, he stays out. Lombard, you must have shortened his life with the shock. Any fingerprints on that bottle of mine? Apart from mine, of course."

"I hope so. I am taking it to the police this morning and we shall hear in due course if not sooner, and I only hope there will be something to hear. They will probably want your prints for elimination purposes."

"They shall have them," said Hambledon cheerfully, "whenever they like to ask." He stood up and looked at himself in the mirror. "My gosh, I look like a picture on a temperance tract, 'What You'll Look Like If You Keep On.' See you later."

They went down separately to breakfast and sat in their usual places at opposite corners of the dining room. They finished at different times and each strolled out alone to take the morning air, wander round the little town, and stare in at the shopwindows. It so happened that they were both in the Bahnhofstrasse, Hambledon coming out of the post office and Lombard looking at watches in the window of Richard Wagner the clockmaker, when Horaz came up the street.

He was leading one of the Tyrol's endearing bullocks in an oxcart loaded with logs, a long, low, narrow cart with four wooden wheels and outward-sloping sides of unpainted wooden slats, widely spaced. The cart had one shaft only, on the bullock's right side; his harness consisted mainly of a flat leather collar to which the traces were attached and a headstall with a rope to lead him by. This looks a one-sided arrangement, but the Tyrolese draught oxen are presumably used to it and do not, apparently, object.

Horaz looked, if possible, even more vacant than he had when he carried Hambledon's luggage from the station. His appearance was rather improved than otherwise by bright patches of green and tawny lichen which the logs had deposited upon his clothes, and the broken tip of his hat-feather swung loosely at every step. The equipage attracted some natural attention from passing visitors, but Horaz took no notice at all of their interested glances or even of a cine-camera which was trained upon him. Hambledon, standing at the edge of the pavement, saw plainly that the lobe of his left ear was scratched and swollen and that he had the beginnings of a wonderful black eye.

It will be remembered that when the proprietor of Der Schwartzhund in Basle called in the police, they found in his back room two men who could not tell them anything, for they were both dead. The Russian, Alexis Medeski, who had also been there, had left before they arrived; now he returned with rapid steps to his own hotel where he went straight up to his room, sat down upon the bed, and took his head in both hands.

He had been sent to buy the guided missile details from the Frenchman and had lost them.

He had been provided with the money to pay for them and he had lost that too. The Russians are well known to be highly intolerant of incompetence in their emissaries and they would not regard sympathetically any such story as he had to tell. They might not even believe it; there was a very substantial sum of money involved. Medeski thought this over for a few minutes and the thought made his head ache; he flung the window wide open, bathed his face in cold water, and sat down again.

His head cleared. The money was quite unimportant if he could regain the papers; his Government had been perfectly willing to pay it out and would not care in the least who had it so long as they received the papers in exchange. He could forget the money and concentrate on the papers, and here he had an advantage which the gang who had robbed him did not know he possessed. He had recogized the man who had committed the robbery.

About two years earlier, when Medeski first came to Berne, there had been a small affair in which it was found advisable to employ one or two persons whose undoubted ability, resource, and experience were not equalled by their ethical standards. In a word, crooks. The interview with their representative was conducted by one of Medeski's superiors. The meeting took place at an open-air café by the lakeside at Zurich, and Medeski had been sent to sit at a table near enough to see what happened in case there was any trouble. There was not, but he saw the leader and remembered not only his face but his name, Eugene. At least, that was the name he had given though it sounded a little incomplete.

Negotiations for meeting Eugene had been made through a man in Innsbruck whose name was—was——

"Now, do not panic," said Medeski, addressing himself aloud. "Let the mind relax, let it merely float back to those days and the name will rise to the surface of its own accord. I am calm and resolute. I am not either frightened or excited. This opportunity—at first sight, distressing affair—has come to enable me to prove my worth to my Embassy. I might even get promotion at its successful conclusion."

He rose from the edge of his bed, took his coat off to brush it carefully, and put on a clean collar. When he was tidy and ready once more to face the world he looked critically at himself in the long mirror of his wardrobe; no one who looked less like a desperate and ruthless man could possibly be imagined. He was short and small-boned, neither fat nor thin, with dark hair brushed smoothly back and a round face with unremarkable features. He was dressed in a well-fitting dark suit, his tie showed a neat pattern in three shades of grey, and he wore a small dark moustache. He might have been a bank cashier of the utmost respectability. He was not of any particular racial type though anyone asked to guess at his nationality might have suggested that he was French. He stood and looked at himself in the mirror, picking from his coatcollar a tiny speck of fluff which had evaded the clothesbrush, while all the time through the background of his mind there flowed an idle stream of recollections of those thrilling days two years ago when first he left his native land to come to the Embassy at Berne, the lectures and admonitions designed to render him proof against the deceits and temptations of the West—the West—the North——

"Norz," he said aloud, and his expressionless face actually creased into a smile. "Norz."

The smile faded abruptly when he remembered that he was due to report back to Berne before noon the next day, bearing the designs with him, those few flimsy sheets of incredibly thin paper upon which his eyes had exultantly rested only to see them vanish again in a moment of violence; a strong smell of cordite and that Frenchman's head with one side blown away; Eugene with a smoking gun; and that other man dragging in the body of Gregor, dripping blood. No use looking for Eugene in Basle; he would be out of the city before his gun had cooled.

Medeski crossed the room and sat down under the light to consult a railway timetable.

He reached Innsbruck in the afternoon of the following day, several hours before Hambledon himself did so, but there Medeski's inspiration deserted him. When one does not know where a man lives and is afraid to ask for him by name, the search for him is apt to be slow and difficult. Medeski suffered from frustration as well as by terror for three interminable days

until at last someone hinted obscurely that if the Herr wanted
to get into touch with the sort of persons who did not like having
their names bandied about, the place to go was a certain café
in a back street behind the shunting-yards of Innsbruck's goods
station.

Medeski hurried to it and found it a squalid place frequented
by men who looked at him with open distrust and who, with
one accord, fell silent when he went in; the landlord, behind the
bar, was an enormous man with one walleye and a mouth like
a rattrap. The place and its clients alike had a sinister air and
Medeski all but turned on his heel to go out again. However,
he was desperate by that time and desperation made him bold.
He walked across the watching, silent room and spoke to the
man behind the bar.

"I am looking for a friend," said Medeski. "I have been told
that you can help me."

The landlord brought out, from under the counter, a grimy
damp rag with which he began to rub the top of the bar. He
made no answer, merely glancing at Medeski occasionally with
the one clear eye. The Russian felt a chilly sensation run down
his spine, this bar-rubbing might perhaps be some kind of signal.
He glanced over his shoulder but none of the men had moved.

"I have been asked," continued Medeski in a lower voice, "by
someone who owes him money to try to find him in order that
the debt may be paid."

Still no answer, only the slow sweeping strokes with the stained
rag.

"It will be a pity," persisted Medeski, "if you cannot help me.
I have come from Basle to find my friend."

The landlord stopped rubbing, looked Medeski straight in the
face, and then nodded towards a little man who was sitting alone
at a table in a corner. Medeski walked across to it, drew out a
chair with a murmur of apology, and sat down; even as he did
so the landlord appeared at his elbow, set down two glasses of
red wine upon the table and stood waiting. Medeski gave him
a note considerably in excess of the price of the wine; if he
expected change he was disappointed for the man merely took
the money and walked quietly away.

Medeski pushed one glass across the table, picked up his own and said, "*Salut!*" The little man put out a skinny hand—he was small and skinny in every way; he might have been a jockey— murmured, "*Salut!*" in reply and drank from his glass. "I thank the Herr," he added.

Medeski nodded, sipped from his own glass, decided that the wine was a mixture of red ink and methylated spirit with possibly a dash of sulphuric acid, and set the glass down again to lean forward across the table.

"I am looking for a friend," he said. "I think that perhaps you can help me to find him."

The little man's eyebrows went up. "How could that be?" he asked simply. "I am not likely to know any of the Herr's friends."

"It would be a pity if you could not help me. I have been asked to find him by someone who owes him money in order that the debt may be paid."

The man giggled and Medeski asked what amused him.

"For me," he explained, "if I owe a man money he comes to look for me, in my experience. I do not have to look for him."

"This is different," said Medeski sternly. "It is, in this case, a debt of honour, if you know what that is."

"No. Among us, we do not have such things."

"I daresay not," said Medeski condescendingly. "Never mind. Will you help me?"

"How can I, when I do not know your friend's name?"

"Norz," said Medeski in a low voice.

"He is not at home at present," said the little man, after a pause. "He is in retirement just now."

"Of course I knew that," said Medeski, who did not know any- thing of the kind. "That is why I appeal to you."

"I cannot tell you where he is——"

"But——"

"But I can take you there."

"Admirable," said Medeski enthusiastically. "I assure you that he will be delighted to see me. Shall we go?"

They went, accordingly; as Medeski turned in the doorway to shut the door he saw with some uneasiness the landlord's one clear eye fixed unwaveringly upon him and it came into his mind that he had been expected, or recognized, or both. He shut the door hastily and walked away with the little man, who chattered as they went.

"Herr Norz," he said, "is a great man in his line, but of course you will know that already. He is very deeply engaged, always, in most important affairs. I do not, myself, know anything about his affairs and if I did of course I would not speak of them. I count myself lucky to be asked to do small things for him sometimes, such as opening a tiresome lock or keeping watch for someone. He trusts me."

"I am sure," said Medeski politely, "that his trust is not misplaced."

"You may be sure of that. That is why I made a long study of you before I agreed to take you to him. You may have thought it rude. I am sorry, but I have to be careful."

"Of course. You were quite right. You are working for him now, I gather."

"At the moment," said the little man with a laugh of quite genuine amusement, "it is something very simple. I am, as you might say, his housekeeper."

"Housekeeper!"

"That is, I do his shopping, buy his groceries, his wine, all that he wants and take it to him. For, as the Herr will agree, a man may be in hiding, but he must still eat and drink. Eh? And I have to pay for everything, too, though I tell him that there is no need. I could bring him the pick of half the delicatessen shops in Innsbruck and the proprietors would be none the wiser. But no, he is no petty thief, he says, so I must take the money and pay and keep account and bring back the change. It is amusing, that?"

"Very amusing," said Medeski gravely.

"I find it so. Every day, when I bring back his change, I laugh about it. Well, here we are. Down these steps. Shall I lead the way?"

They were in a quarter of the town which is a maze of narrow alleys between dark ancient houses whose gables seemed to lean forward to whisper to each other; houses where grimy windows, flaking paint, and rotting woodwork proclaimed that, if once they were fine, they were now slum tenements and nothing more. The little man turned into a deep doorway upon a paved entry, lit only by one bare electric light bulb, from which stone stairs went up many stories above and also down below pavement level. He went down the stairs and Medeski followed closely at his heels.

"Careful here; the bottom step is broken, and there is no electric light down here. This is the door."

It was light enough for Medeski to see that the door was very old, immensely strong, and studded with iron nails. His guide tapped upon it in a pattern of knocks, plainly prearranged, and a voice within asked who was there.

"Me."

"And who the devil is 'me'?"

"Klaus, of course," said the little man in a pained voice. "Who else would it be?"

There came the sound of elaborate unfastening; a lock turned cumbrously, bolts slid back, and sliding noises suggested additional bars. At last the door opened narrowly, Klaus slipped through, politely held it for Medeski, and shut it behind him. Klaus turned with a pleased smile on his face which changed abruptly to a look of horror.

Medeski, with his back to the wall, had a gun in his hand.

CHAPTER X

By Candlelight

For an instant, while a man's pulse might beat twice, the scene was still as a picture. There were two men in the room, two chairs and a table with a lighted candle upon it. Hambledon would have recognized both men; they were Norz and his servant Hugo.

"Sit down in the chairs," barked Medeski, "both of you. Klaus, fasten the door. I am very willing to kill any or all of you."

The two men sat down and remained perfectly still; only their eyes glittered in the candlelight as Medeski's gun weaved back and forth from one to the other. Klaus, whimpering with terror, locked and bolted the door and slid two stout iron bars into place, they reached from one doorpost to the other. When he had finished he turned round, still holding the bar with one hand as though his knees were giving way, and his face was pallid and glistening.

Medeski, using his left hand, drew a hank of thin cord from his pocket and tossed it to Klaus.

"Now tie them to their chairs. First their ankles to each front leg——"

"Oh no," wailed Klaus, "not my Herr——"

"Do you want to die?" asked Medeski softly and his eyelids drooped over his eyes till they looked like the eyes of a lizard, dull and cold.

"No, no——"

"Get on. First their ankles to each front leg. There is an old knife, I notice, on the table. You may use that to cut the cord. No, tighter than that. Get on."

"Forgive, Herr Norz, forgive!"

But Norz never moved nor spoke, and the wretched Klaus went on with his task, prompted by Medeski.

"Since these inferior chairs have no arms, you may tie their wrists down to the back legs. At full stretch, if you please. Now a cord right round their chests and the backs of the chairs. Tighter than that."

At last the task was done. Klaus stood up and said, "Please, may I go now?"

"No. Just a moment. Is there any back way out of this place?"

Klaus was about to answer when a wordless growl from Norz stopped him.

"Answer!" said Medeski.

"I don't know."

Medeski raised his gun and levelled it at Klaus.

"Yes—yes, there is. At the back, up there." Medeski walked forward and looked up.

"But there is a grating over it."

"It—it isn't fastened. It hinges. It is in case the police break down the door."

Medeski looked at the door with its great lock a foot square, its heavy bolts at the top and the bottom, and the iron bars over all.

"I should think it would take even the police some time to break down that door."

"Please," said Klaus, "may I go now?"

"One more thing. Take their shoes and socks off."

"Take off their——"

"Shoes and socks, fool. Be quick, I am in a hurry."

Klaus obeyed, first Norz and then Hugo. He was kneeling with his back to Medeski drawing off Hugo's second sock when the Russian spoke again.

"That is right. Now I do not think I have any further use for you."

He turned his gun in his hand, holding it by the barrel, and struck savagely at the kneeling man's head with the butt. Klaus grunted once and rolled over unconscious.

"So much for your jackal. Now, gentlemen, I have a question to ask you and I should like an immediate and truthful answer." Medeski looked around. "What, only two chairs and my hosts occupying both of them? That is not good manners, but perhaps you will say it is my fault. We will excuse it, under the circumstances." He pulled up a stool and sat down on it. "I will make myself quite clear. Your organization has stolen from me some copies of a design of an American war weapon." Medeski paused, drew his forces together, and spoke with a concentrated menace all the more terrifying from one who looked like a suburban bank clerk. "You are going to return those papers to me *at once.*"

Norz said, "We have not got them."

"Your organization has got them."

"No," said Norz. "That is not true."

Medeski looked at him for a long moment, sighed, and said, "Very well. If you prefer to be obstinate——"

He picked up the lighted candle and went down on one knee before Norz's chair as Klaus had done——

Norz writhed and cursed and Medeski drew back.

"Where are those papers?"

Norz did not answer.

"What, you want some more? Curious. People do not, as a rule, ask for more of this. However, if you insist——"

Norz began shouting at the top of his voice for the police, police! Police!

"You make too much noise," said Medeski, putting the candle back on the table. He was quite right. There were two constables passing at that moment, two because in that area they patrol in pairs. They heard the cry and stopped.

"Was that," said one, "somebody calling us?"

"Surely not," said the other. "Such a thing is not done in this part of the town, as you know."

"If it was, it may be a trap," said the first constable cautiously. "I think we had better disregard——"

"*Police!*"

"That sounded almost genuine," said the second constable in a surprised voice.

"It did, and it came from that basement."

"*Police!*"

"We had better go down, but be careful. Come on." They turned in by the deep archway and looked suspiciously about them. "Down here."

"Since you will not talk by method one," said Medeski, "we must try method two." He took a clasp knife from his pocket and opened the biggest blade; it was new and glittered evilly in the candlelight. It looked horribly sharp and Norz shrank in his chair.

There came the sound of heavy knocking and voices, muffled by the thick door. "Open! Police! Open!"

"There," gasped Norz.

"That will not help you," said Medeski. "It will take them half an hour to break that door in, and I can seriously inconvenience you in ten seconds. You see this knife, yes? Now, for this method I must undo the lower buttons of your waistcoat. Excuse me."

"Stop! Stop, stop! I'll tell you. We had your papers but not for long. They were stolen from us, an Englishman has them."

"An Englishman? Where has he taken them? To England?"

"No, no. He has them with him, we are sure of that. He is at Seefeld."

"At Seefeld! What is his name?"

"Hambledon," gasped Norz. "At the Karwendelhof, at Seefeld."

"If you have lied to me," said Medeski, "I will come back. Then you will wish you were dead. Then, a long time after, you will get your wish."

When the police eventually broke down the door in reply to Norz's repeated appeals, since in jail he would be safe from Medeski, they found, tied to chairs, two men for whom they had been looking for two days. One of them had a bandage round his arm and required more on his feet. There was also, upon the floor, the unconscious form of a petty crook. The police looked round the room.

"Someone else," they said, "has been here."

"Marvellous," said Norz. "How did you guess?"

Hambledon strolled across the square and admired *lederhosen* and knitted pullovers of elaborate pattern in the window of the

Sporthaus Schöpf. Lombard, also idly windowshopping, wandered up to stand beside him.

"Horaz," said Hambledon in a low tone, "has a sore ear and the beginnings of a fine black eye."

"It was not Horaz in your room last night," answered Lombard. "I saw his back in the passage light as he went out, smooth brown hair cut very short and a stiff white collar. Not the same shape and moved differently."

"There's one odd thing about Horaz," persisted Hambledon.

"Only one?"

"He is always so neatly shaved."

"To settle the doubts which I perceive the Herr to entertain," said Lombard precisely, "I will make a few enquiries about what, if anything except sleeping, Horaz was doing last night. He may have been chopping wood and a piece flew up and hit him."

He drifted away to look into the other window. Rain was beginning to fall and Hambledon, who had come out without a raincoat, turned up his collar and went back to the Karwendelhof with long strides. There are no half measures about rain in the mountains when it comes on suddenly. He ran the last fifty yards and ducked under the shelter of the porch to find the entrance hall full of more or less damp people who had been caught out as he was. Among them was Agatha Wiggins, the gawky woman who had come to his table in the Karwendelkeller the evening before.

"Dear Mr. Hambledon! What a downpour!"

"Yes, isn't it?" said Tommy, circling round her. "I am just going up to change my coat, the shoulders are wet."

"I saw it coming," she said, "and got in before it started."

"Splendid," said Tommy, backing away towards the stairs.

"I think it has set in for the day. Just a short moment, there was something I wanted to ask you."

He stopped, of course, and began dabbing with his handkerchief at the raindrops on his sleeves.

"Do you think you could possibly lend me a book to read? The papers are all being read by different people and I am lost, Mr. Hambledon, completely lost without anything to read!"

"I am so sorry," he said, "I haven't got one. I never carry books about with me."

"Oh dear! I'm so sorry. I suppose the one on your bedside table is one somebody has lent you."

"On my bedside table——"

Two young girls standing within earshot became afflicted with giggles and moved hastily away while Miss Wiggins broke into a silvery laugh.

"I do apologize," she said. "The remark did sound a little ambiguous, did it not? What actually happened was that I was passing your room this morning when the chambermaid was making the bed, and I just glanced in in passing, as one does, you know, and there was a book on the bedside table. That was why I ventured to ask you, because I knew you had one."

"Oh, that," said Tommy. "I don't think you'd care for that; it's a book I picked up in the train. It's a handbook about making model galleons, that's all. It isn't what you might call a reading book——"

"Oh, but I adore model galleons! I have even made one or two all by myself. With construction kits, you know."

"I'll bring it down," said Tommy, and went upstairs two steps at a time. "Aggie, the human emu," he commented to himself, for the emu is one of the silliest-looking birds there is and has also a long thin neck and a long beak. Nonetheless, he took the book with him when he went down, since a promise is a promise. It was received with chirps of joy, and Miss Wiggins actually went away in order to sit down quietly and read it.

When Lombard came in Hambledon was standing at one of the windows watching the raindrops chasing each other down the panes, and it was only natural for another hotel guest to come up and exchange remarks about the weather.

"You would never think that there were any mountains behind that cloud bank," he said, coming close to the window to look up at the sky. "Horaz," he added in a low voice, "got a bit tight last night and made a nuisance of himself at a dance in one of the smaller places here. So the management threw him out, although, as I understand, he did not wish to go. The head waiter's nose is swollen."

"Oh, really. That seems to settle it, doesn't it? Yes, somehow that sort of behaviour doesn't sound like Horaz, does it? He does not seem quite the type to go to dances, somehow."

"It's much more the sort of thing Horaz would do than to creep into a hotel bedroom in the night to hunt for stolen designs," said Lombard decisively. "I know my countrymen better than you do, believe me. If a cowherd or a baker's assistant took a fancy to go to a dance, he would wash his face, brush his hair, put on a clean shirt, and go. Why not? Austrians have naturally good manners and most of them seem able to dance."

"No doubt," said Hambledon. "Why not, indeed? I'm sure you're right. But Horaz——"

"I think you have—what is the English saying? A wasp in your hair?—about Horaz. There is not the slightest evidence that he is not what he seems: a countryman, a little simple. What have you against him?"

"Nothing, really," admitted Tommy. "Only a dim feeling in the back of my mind that he is a little bigger than life-size."

Lombard looked at him curiously. "It's an odd thing, but your saying that does impress me. I know these unfounded warnings one gets about apparently harmless people and there's usually something in them. We'll have him watched, then, if you insist. But why don't I feel it too?"

"I am probably leading you up the garden path."

"A pleasant place for a walk," said Lombard. "I think the rain is stopping, I shall go out."

After dinner that evening Hambledon was standing in the hall wondering whether he would go out, since the weather was repentant, or go down to the *Keller* for an hour or so, when he found himself addressed by Agatha Wiggins.

"Dear Mr. Hambledon! I must thank you so much for lending me that book. Most interesting. It makes my fingers itch to close round my tools and get down to it with one of those enchanting models."

"So glad," said Tommy, stepping back.

"Are you going down to the *Keller* tonight?"

"I am not sure," he said truthfully. "There might——"

"A most exciting thing happened last night, I must tell you about it. Soon after dear Colonel and Mrs. Grantham went up to bed and you went off to talk to someone at the bar, I and some friends decided to go out to one of those little places where there are not so many tourists. It is nice sometimes, is it not, to get away from the visitors and see the local inhabitants enjoying themselves among their own friends? One feels so much more nearly in touch with the people."

"Undoubtedly. Undoubtedly."

"So I took them along to a little place I have been to once or twice on previous visits and we just sat quietly together with a glass of wine watching the boys and girls enjoying themselves with their interesting traditional dances."

"It must," said Tommy, edging away, "have been quite a thrill."

"And it was all so pleasant and homely when all of a sudden the door positively burst open and a man came in rather drunk and began to interfere with the dancers. Pulling the girls away from their partners, laughing loudly, and making rather Anglo-Saxon remarks if you know what I mean, Mr. Hambledon. Of course, they were all talking German which I understand quite well."

"Under the circumstances perhaps that was a pity," said Tommy, no longer attempting to get away. "What happened next?"

"Oh, the management tried to persuade him to go away but he wouldn't, so they put him out. Threw him out on his ear, they say, do they not? There was quite a fight for a few minutes, and the headwaiter had to retire, holding a handkerchief to his nose. Poor man, it must have hurt. So painful, a bump on the nose."

"Yes, indeed it is. They got rid of the fellow in the end, I suppose?"

"Oh yes, and I must say the manager came and apologized quite charmingly to us for there having been a disturbance when we had been so good as to honour them with our presence, and so on. Quite delightful, he was. I was quite touched. He said that of course the man would never be allowed in there again. Apparently he is a little mentally subnormal. You may have seen the man, he is always about. Tall and skinny, with a long nose and an awful hat with a long feather at the back, very shabby. I call him the Pied Piper."

"I know the man you mean."

"He must have had quite an evening out," said Miss Wiggins, laughing merrily, "because, do you know, he had been fighting somewhere else before that, for his left eye was red and badly swollen and one of his ears had been damaged."

"Really? Are you sure of that?"

"Oh, quite sure, quite. He passed close by our table when he came in and I remarked to my friends that there was a man who would have a black eye in the morning, and that was before the fight started. Odd, wasn't it, that he should have wanted to fight again?"

"One of those whom drink renders pugnacious, evidently," said Hambledon severely. "I am sorry that you should have witnessed such an unpleasant scene."

"Oh, I did not mind, really! I am quite an experienced traveller."

There was a general drift towards the *Keller* as the time came for the dancing to start. Hambledon managed to lose the lady and slipped off to find Lombard.

"Well now," said Hambledon, when he had passed on this piece of information, "do you still think your Horaz is the harmless yokel he looks?"

Lombard hesitated. "I still find it very hard to believe that Horaz was the man I scrapped with in your bedroom. I saw him —only his back, it's true—when he went out and that man was quite a different type. You are arguing that he got himself involved in a second scrap to account for the marks he got in the first, but we don't know that Horaz didn't have two fights that night, do we? Horaz as himself, I mean. Drink does turn some men into tigers; he might have had half-a-dozen scraps without our knowing it."

Hambledon shrugged his shoulders.

"But I tell you what we'll do," said Lombard. "We'll go tomorrow and have a look at that hut of his. I know which one it is."

In the antique shop of A. G. Eisenschmidt in Lieberstrasse, Innsbruck, the elderly Herr Eisenschmidt still pottered round dusting, rubbing up the furniture, and occasionally altering the arrangement of the window. He had a fair number of customers since it was the holiday season, but his most persistent visitors were the police.

They had, very naturally, descended upon the place in some force, together with cameramen, fingerprint experts, and other specialists, directly after Lombard had returned to Innsbruck police station after rescuing Hambledon from Norz's spirited attempt to drown him in the river Inn. The police were principally concerned with Norz's flat on the first floor which they occupied all day and sealed up at night, but they naturally had a great number of questions to ask the aged Herr below. They did not learn a great deal from him.

He did not know anything about the antecedents of Herr Norz. Why should he? The young man did not confide in him; there was no reason why he should. When Eisenschmidt dropped deeper and deeper into financial difficulties—"for who buys valuable furniture and *objets d'art* during such a war? People sell their valuables; they do not buy." The police nodded; they knew it was true. "I—to tell you truth—I was hungry, often. I would look round my shop and see this worth six hundred schillings, that worth two thousand, that worth seventeen hundred, but I could not eat them. I give the butcher, the baker little silver pieces, small jewels, a little picture for meat and bread until they will take no more. They cannot sell either, if no one will buy. So I run into debt, and all the time I am getting older and older."

The police shifted their feet and made sympathetic noises.

"So, just when I think I can go on no longer but must crawl away somewhere to die, comes this young man and says: 'I will buy your place outright. I want the house to live in myself. You must find somewhere else to live.' He is brusque in manner but his money is all right; yes, yes, I asked my bank to look into that. My bank, it had been my bank when I had occasion for one, looked into this affair for me out of kindness since I had known them these many years. So he paid me and I paid my debts and looked round for somewhere to sit down and wait for death. For indeed, gentlemen, he had a bargain.

The old gentleman sighed heavily and wiped his eyes.

"Well then, I was packing up to go I knew not where, when

one day he came striding up the stairs there—he did not even knock, but after all it was his house—and said: 'Old man, if you wish, you can stay on to keep the shop. You know more about the trade than I do, and I do not suppose you will cheat me more than another man.' Gentlemen, for a moment the strength flowed back into me and I could have thrown him down the stairs, but I remembered that I had taken his money and much of it was already spent. Besides, this," he waved his hand round the shop, "is my life; it is to die one death to leave it. So I agreed, and he pays me a salary and checks very carefully my accounts, and I live in a room near by. But you will understand that we are not," he laughed a little, "cordially intimate. He has the separate stair to his apartment and once a month we meet and go through the accounts."

"So you know nothing of who his friends are, who visits him, where he goes——"

"Gentlemen, for the most part I do not even know whether he is here or not unless I hear that oaf of a servant stamping about overhead. Yes, I mislead you. Occasionally, when I know he is at home, I ask for an interview and say: 'There is a sale, Herr Norz, at such a house, or so-and-so in Lucerne or Munich has some things for disposal. I wish to close the shop for two days and go to see them, with your permission.' He never refuses. He says: 'Inform the police you will be away. I cannot be your watchdog. Put a notice in the window. I cannot have fools banging upon my door.' I say: 'Very good, Herr Norz,' and leave him. Your records, gentlemen, will perhaps show how often I have done this in the past ten years or so. I cannot remember."

He leaned back in his chair with a weary sigh and the police left him for the time.

"Poor old boy," said one. "Can't stand the man Norz at any price, can he?"

"I don't wonder! Surly brute, Norz, by his account."

After Norz and Hugo had been found in the cellar where Medeski had left them, the police went back to Eisenschmidt to try to clear up a few more points but found him definitely unhelpful.

"I know nothing! Nothing! I told you before, all I knew. I must beg that you will not come here any oftener than is con-

sistent with your absolute duty. For one thing, it is bad for
business. Customers do not care to enter a shop infested with
police; they think there is something wrong with it."

"And your other reason?"

The old man fidgeted.

"They are bad men, I understand. Dangerous criminals, are
they not? I am fraid, if they think I have been chattering to the
police—I am afraid, I tell you. Please go away."

CHAPTER XI

The Little Hut

Horaz's hut was at the top of a field beside the road to Mosern. It was backed by woods and looked over the little Lake Chapel in the valley. Hambledon arranged to meet Lombard by the chapel, since they did not wish to be seen walking through the village together. When Tommy arrived he found Lucius Lombard waiting for him.

"Have you seen Horaz this morning?" he asked. "I have not."

"I have," said Hambledon. "He went over the level-crossing towards the Wald Hotel carrying a laundry basket. It seemed heavy."

"It could not be better arranged if we had sent him that way ourselves," said Lombard. "Shall we go, then?"

The woods behind the hut are intersected with numerous paths, nor is that hillside so steep as to make it ncessary to remain upon them. The two men circled round behind the hut and came upon it from the back. Since these huts are intended to contain hay, none of them are fitted with windows and this one was no exception. It was fairly new and sturdily built of planks. There was one large door which was not only firmly closed but locked with a strong new padlock.

"He does not mean to be burgled," said Hambledon. "Look, the hasp for the padlock is not screwed on the door, it is bolted on. No use trying to take that off."

"A pity," said Lombard wistfully. "I brought a screw driver."

"I brought something better than that," said Hambledon, and took from his pocket the sort of small leather case which usually contains a manicure set; he opened it to show Lombard that it contained a set of picklocks, a pair of pliers more like a dentist's forceps than the innocent implement of the household toolbox, one or two small but strong levers, a glazier's diamond, and a magnet.

"That," said Lombard admiringly, "is quite the neatest set of burglar's tools I have ever seen."

"It belongs to quite a neat burglar," explained Tommy, "but he doesn't want it at the moment; he's in Dartmoor. At least," he added, taking out the picklocks and starting operations on the padlock, "I expect he really wants them rather badly, but it is thought better that he should not have them just now." There was a loud click and the padlock opened. "Well, if there aren't any booby traps, spring guns, bombs, savage dogs, or chained tigers inside, shall we go in?"

"Allow me," said Lombard politely, and opened the door. Since nothing bit them, shot at them, or dropped nooses over their heads they went in.

"Better shut the door," said Lombard; "it might attract attention, standing open."

"It will be dark," said Hambledon.

"Not when I have switched on my torch," said Lombard, with dignity. "There is not one in your kit, is there?"

He threw the beam round the inside of the hut and Hambledon uttered an exclamation.

"Here's a motorcycle, and quite a good one."

"Probably his pride and joy," said Lombard, "or it may not be his; he may be housing it for somebody."

"It seems to me to be an odd thing for your poverty-stricken yokel to possess, don't you agree? But one must be fair, however much the effort costs one. Perhaps he won it in a raffle."

Lombard laughed and made a note of the number.

"Not much else here, by the look of it," said Hambledon, "and I think we'd better not loiter too long. Primus stove—Miss Wiggins was quite right—a few simple groceries, a shabby suitcase not even locked containing underwear and shirts, a few kitchen utensils, and a sack or two of chaff which I take to be his bed. A couple of rugs—what's this hanging on the wall? A suit, Lombard, quite a good one. Let's go, shall we? I'm getting fidgety and that's always a sign of something though I am never sure what. Motorcyclist's overalls—oh, come on."

They went out quickly, locked up after them, and took to the woods again. Five minutes later Lombard, leading the way, stopped suddenly where a gap in the trees showed a short length of the Mosern road. A tall thin figure was coming up it, shambling at the knees in a long, deceptively slow stride, and the broken tip of the tall thin hat-feather waggled absurdily at every stride.

"There's no doubt," said Lombard after a prolonged pause, "the Herr has intuitions."

"I know I have," said Hambledon anxiously, "but I should dearly like to know whether Horaz has, too."

"What I want to know," said Hambledon, on the following morning, "is why this gang keep on chasing me for those papers? If they had some absurd reason for thinking I had them at one time, why do they suppose I have still got them with me? I wouldn't keep such papers about me. I should send them away by post or whistle up a Queen's Messenger or something practical like that. Certainly not put them in the hotel safe."

For the Karwendelhof's safe, which stands behind the reception desk in the entrance hall, had been opened during the night and searched. Nothing seemed to have been taken, not even money, but all the contents had been pulled out, dropped in a confused mass on the floor, and left there for somebody else to clear up. Even the safe door had been left standing open. Since there was nothing missing, the management had kept the distressing affair a secret from its guests and even Hambledon knew nothing about it till Lombard told him.

"They came and woke me up," said Lombard, "soon after half past five this morning. Of course, the management know what my real job is though they keep it to themselves. I imagine the gang thought they would just make sure the papers were not there. I do not suppose they really expected to find them."

"Any fingerprints?"

"Certainly not. Do you take them for amateurs?"

"No."

"And you are quite right," said Lombard. "As for their thinking you still have the papers, you do not realize what they take you for. They do not know you are a high-ranking British official; they think you are a crook on the make. What is more, if, when they were searching, they came across that charming little burglar's kit of yours, they will be quite sure they are right."

"Yes, I daresay. I wonder, you know, that they didn't take that while they were about it."

"Perhaps they have even better ones of their own. As for the papers, if you were a crook dealing in that sort of merchandise, you would not part with them. You would not trust anyone sufficiently. They are immensely valuable. You would not even trust the post supposing that you could think of someone to send them to. You would either keep them on you or hide them somewhere so silly that no one would think of looking there for them."

"Such as pasting them up on the town notice board," suggested Hambledon.

"Yes. Have you any idea what they look like?"

"No. Copies of this highly secret missile were made and smuggled out of the office, so they can't be large rolls such as architects carry about under their arms, to take an extreme example. I imagine they would be small enough—or on thin enough paper—to go in somebody's inside breast pocket without making it bulge noticeably, but that's only my common sense talking, not my knowledge."

"I understand. In point of fact, you and I have quite different objects in view in this affair. I want to rope in this gang of criminals and especially their leader. I have not been asked to look for the designs and I have plenty of things in my life to afford me interest and amusement without getting excited over a set of drawings which will probably be obsolete in a year's time when somebody else has invented something worse."

"You are quite right. I sincerely hope you catch your rogues and I will help you if I can, but my job is to find those infernal designs. My Department is getting fidgety about them. I think life is sometimes a little unfair," said Tommy plaintively. "Here

am I being harassed by a gang of thugs because they think I
have got the papers and getting rockets from my Department
because I have not got the papers and all the time I have not
the faintest shadow of an idea where they are. I am not even
convinced that they still exist. Bastien may have destroyed them
when he found himself headed off at Calais. He had several
hours there between trains and I don't know what he did or
where he went. They were pretty hot, you know, he may have
found them too hot to handle; his most sensible course would
have been to retire into seclusion, burn them and wash away
the ashes."

"The gang don't think he did——"

"My dear Lombard, the gang think I've got them. That's
what their brains are worth. I think I shall go out and look for
edelweiss or chamois. It's a lovely morning."

"Have you got a pair of binoculars?"

"Whatever for? To look for edelweiss?"

"No, no. Although you might find them a help with the chamois.
No, I was going to ask you whether, if you had, you would lend
them to me for the day. I think I shall go and lie up on the
hillside somewhere and keep a distant watch upon that hut of
Horaz's. I've stupidly left mine at home and I cannot receive
them earlier than tomorrow."

"Certainly you shall have them. Will you come along to my
room?"

"Thank you, in a few minutes I will. I am just going down to
see if there are any letters in for me."

Lombard came up five minutes later and Hambledon looked
at him.

"Years ago," he said, "when I was a small boy we had a cat
which found out how to open the door of the meat-safe. You
have, at this moment, a look upon your face which reminds me
of the dear departed. How does the catch work?"

Lombard laughed.

"I am not yet so far advanced as that, but I do know the name
of the maker, as one might say. Those prints on the Perrier bottle
in your bedroom, they are Eugene's."

"Eugene. The man who shot the French politician at the
Schwartzhund in Basle and took the papers from a Russian

named Medeski. Incidentally, I wonder what has become of Medeski. Never mind. Have you had an official description of Eugene?"

Lombard handed him a police description of a man about thirty-five years old, brown-haired with grey eyes, long nose, oval face, rounded chin, ears of a certain type, and so on. Height, five feet eleven inches.

"No photograph," said Tommy.

"No. You do not think you have ever seen him?"

"You mean in connection with this case? No, I have not. He was not, for example, Pierre, who shot Bastien in the train, or Norz who tried to——"

"Another piece of news," said Lombard. "Norz has been found and arrested, he and his servant Hugo."

"How very gratifying. When, how, and where?"

"When, last night. How, because he was yelling for the police and they heard him. Where, in a basement room in a slum tenement in Innsbruck. They were tied to chairs and Norz's toes were blistered. With a lighted candle."

"And the man who did it?"

"Skipped by a back way out."

"Dear me," said Hambledon. "Did Norz say who the man was?"

"He said he did not know the man, who gained admission by a trick and tortured them to extort money."

"It's a funny thing," said Hambledon thoughtfully, "that only a moment ago I was wondering aloud what had become of Medeski. This sounds very like him looking for his stolen papers, doesn't it? Did they describe the man?"

"I asked that," said Lombard. "Norz gave a description; so did his servant Hugo and so did also a petty crook who was persuaded to take the man there. The crook was unconscious on the floor when the police broke in, he had been knocked on the head."

"And the descriptions?"

"All three different," said Lombard calmly.

"I wouldn't believe Norz," said Hambledon energetically, "if he told me on oath that December the twenty-fifth was Christmas Day. What do you think about it?"

"If you are right and it was Medeski, I wonder what Norz

told him before the police arrived. Did he say 'Your missing papers are in the possession of a certain Englishman staying at Seefeld'?"

Hambledon burst into laughter.

"I was complaining just now because I was being chased up by my Department and by your gang. Dammit, people are queuing up to get after me. I suppose if Medeski—if it was he—does go into action, we shall notice something happening. Let's have a nice quiet morning before it all starts, shall we? Here are my field glasses. We'll both go and watch Horaz's hut; we may not have leisure enough, later."

They met by arrangement in the woods behind the hut, found a sunny outcrop from which they could look down upon the hut, themselves unnoticeable, and settled down to wait.

It was not until after three in the afternoon that Hambledon, placidly asleep in the sun, was awakened by Lombard's hand upon his ankle. Horaz was walking up the field towards his hut; he unlocked the door and went in, shutting it behind him, and another half hour passed.

The hut door opened again and a man came out pushing the motorcycle. He was a tall man but otherwise very unlike Horaz; he was square-shouldered and well built; he walked well and held himself like a soldier. It was not possible to see much of his face because he wore a motorcyclist's crash helmet and large tinted-glass goggles, but he was very neat in appearance with none of Horaz's shaggy look, and the dust coat he wore was clean and well-fitting.

"Who the hell's that?" asked Hambledon.

"I don't know. Glasses, quick!" Lombard studied the man carefully and said, "But I think I've seen him. He looks like a man who was standing near you at the bar the other night when you had your drink doped."

"Oh, does he? Let's run after him and snatch his goggles off to see if he's got a black eye, shall we? I wish we weren't so far off, we might have done something. I wonder what—hullo!"

The man leaned the motorcycle against the corner of the hut and went back to shut the door. He was plainly to be seen fitting the padlock into its hasp and locking it, after which he withdrew the key, put it in his pocket, and began to wheel his motorcycle down the field to the gate upon the road. He passed through the gate, mounted his machine, started the engine, and rode away towards Seefeld.

"I must see which road he takes," said Lombard. The little town was sufficiently below them for the streets to be seen, not throughout their length, but at frequent intervals; at crossroads, at the Square, and through gaps between houses the black orb of the crash helmet could be seen getting progressively smaller until it disappeared from sight on the road to Scharnitz.

"I have the number of that machine," said Lombard. "I can find out if he crosses the frontier at Scharnitz."

"In the meantime he has left Horaz locked in. You can't open a padlocked door from inside."

"No. This man was locked in before, though. Horaz unlocked the door when he arrived, if you remember."

"So he did, yes. All this is damn funny, Lombard. Let's go down and ask for a drink of water, you've been taken queer."

"Wait a little. There may be some other way out of the hut, a couple of movable planks, perhaps."

But though they waited for another half hour there was no sign of life from the hut.

"Come on," said Hambledon, getting up, "or that fellow may come back if he's only gone to Scharnitz to buy his groceries."

They went down to the hut and knocked on the door, knocked again and called out, but there was no sign of life nor any movement within.

"Open the door," said Lombard. "That fellow may have killed him."

"I don't think so, myself," said Tommy. "However, we'll just make sure."

He took out his little case and opened the door as before, but the hut was dark, quiet, and unoccupied.

"Your torch a moment, Lombard. What's this hanging up here?"

On a nail above the bed hung something that looked like the top of a man's head.

"Do you know something?" said Tommy Hambledon. "Horaz wears a wig and this is it."

"And the man on the motorcycle——"

"Don't you think that his name is probably Eugene?"

"I wish," said Lombard, "that I'd brought a camera, an insufflator and all the doings for taking fingerprint photographs. I don't like to take anything away, he has so few things here, and if he missed anything he would know that the place had been entered."

"We will call again," said Hambledon soothingly. "If you carried round everything you might need you would want also a small handcart to convey the stuff."

CHAPTER XII

Café Corso

After Medeski's drastic questioning of Norz in the cellar at Innsbruck, he had spent most of the night thinking over what Norz had told him. He had had a good deal of experience, from time to time, of questioning people under torture, and he knew that though it is usually possible to make them talk, it is by no means equally possible to make them speak the truth. They would lie, naturally, and the more quick-witted they were the more convincing the lie would sound, but none the less there was always some little scrap of truth which would slip out while the whirling brain was trying to hold back the important facts in the case. The difficulty was to pick out these grains of truth, but one acquired a certain facility with practice.

In this case it was not even difficult. All that story about the gang having lost the papers to an Englishman named Bumbledom, or something equally silly, who was staying at the Karwendelhof, was obviously a lie, whereas the name Seefeld had an authentic ring about it. It might be that the gang were at or near Seefeld; it was at least worth going there to see. It was pleasant to think that Norz would not be able to warn them of Medeski's coming since he had passed straight from Medeski's hands into those of the police and was no doubt in jail with his toes in bandages. Splendid.

On the other hand, he himself would have to be very careful

indeed upon arrival at Seefeld; he did not know the place, how big it was, or where the gang were, if, indeed, they were there at all. He knew Eugene and had caught a glimpse of Erich at the side door of Der Schwartzhund at Basle; unfortunately Eugene knew Medeski equally well. It would not do to be recognized. A suit of country clothes with suitable accessories, such as the tinted glasses so generally popular, would be advisable. As for the probably nonexistent Englishman at the Karwendelhof, to the devil with him.

Medeski climbed down from the train at Seefeld the following day with a rucksack on his back and a stout walking stick in his hand; he wore a rather loud shirt, a tweed jacket, *lederhosen*, stockings, and stout shoes. On his head was a wide-brimmed brown felt hat with a neat small tuft of feathers at the back; the hat was pulled forward over his eyes which were further protected by tinted glasses with wide dark rims. He did not look much like a native Tyrolese, but he did look very much like many other tourists who are pleased to supplement a change of air with a change of costume. He was very different indeed from the neat little undersecretary of an Embassy, who wore striped trousers, a black jacket, wing collars, and bow ties.

He came out of the station yard with the other passengers and looked about for someone to advise him. He wanted a small *pension* preferably just outside the village, where one could walk out of the door and immediately disappear among the trees; not a large hotel with observant porters and certainly not the Karwendelhof which he saw before him, just across the yard. However, the only local inhabitant who was not labelled for some hotel or travel agency was a gangling yokel in a shocking hat with a broken feather at the back who looked so toothless and silly that Medeski avoided him and walked on down the road. It says a good deal for the respective disguises of Medeski and Horaz-Eugene that neither recognized the other.

With the help of the Travel Bureau, Medeski found a room in a small house on the hillside above the church. The only other visitors in the house were a German honeymoon couple who were all in all to each other, and rightly. It was quite clear that whenever they met the Russian they saw him, if at all, merely as one sees a bright speck in a dusty sunbeam, a thing which has neither substance nor meaning. Medeski for his part always stood aside with lowered eyelids to let them pass upon stairs or in doorways, murmuring, "*'Tag*" or "*'N'amt*," according to the time of day, and not waiting for an answer.

On his first evening he went out for a stroll past the church and into the village with some idea of familiarizing himself with the geography of the place. It might be a good idea to go up to the Travel Bureau and get some walkers' maps of the district. The little town was full of summer visitors, mainly English and German with some Scandinavians. Among so many strangers Medeski attracted no attention from anyone; he was not a noticeable person in any case. He stopped at the crossroads to look into the bright and crowded windows of Scheibner's souvenir shop at the corner; ideologically speaking, he despised this bourgeois nonsense of gaudy scarves, tiny quartered skullcaps with the badge of Seefeld-in-Tyrol, light wrought-iron candlesticks, tooled-leather purses in scarlet and gold, and grotesque carved and painted heads on corks for wine bottles. In theory he despised all this, but in practice there was something cheerful and uplifting in its contemplation; Medeski's normally immobile features nearly softened into a smile.

The pavement is awkardly narrow there; he had to sidle round a group of English girls chattering like starlings together. A motorcycle was coming up to the crossroads; it was on the further side but the road itself is not wide. The rider was wearing a black crash helmet, tinted goggles, and a dust coat; his motorcycle looked expensive, clean, and well-maintained. He was stopped by a big touring coach turning across his bows and Medeski had a good look at him; in spite of the goggles he recognized the rider at once. The road cleared; the motorcyclist pushed off his machine and rode steadily away on the road to Scharnitz.

Medeski's face was once more completely impassive but the heart within him was singing. He had been right, triumphantly right. Norz had indeed let slip the name of Seefeld, for that was Eugene. He was going out of the place; if he lived there he would come back. He had come by that road to the right, probably he lived along there somewhere. He had not come far, for there was no dust upon his boots.

Medeski went up to the Travel Bureau and bought some of the large-scale maps which are sold there for the use of walkers; by this means he learned that the road along which Eugene had come led to Mosern. There did not appear to be many houses along it; it should be possible to find a point of vantage from which one could see where he went. Later that evening, when it was getting dark and Medeski was considering giving it up for the night, the motorcyclist came back along the road, stopped at a field-gate and went through it, pushing his machine up a track through the field to a hut which stood there.

The next day he discovered the identity of Horaz and Eugene. This naturally delighted him when he remembered meeting Horaz face to face at the station when he first arrived, the man had obviously not recognized him. This was magnificent. Medeski knew Horaz-Eugene and was himself unknown, a very strong position. He was a little puzzled by two men who also appeared to be taking an interest in Horaz's hut one afternoon but he did not see them again. Tourists, probably, just nosing about. Medeski had lost interest in the hut by that time; he was watching the Scharnitz road.

It was becoming increasingly difficult for Hambledon and Lombard to meet for consultation without being seen together, except in their respective bedrooms at night. Tommy was, therefore, very pleased when he discovered the Café Corso. This is entered through a romantic-looking deep stone archway in the Bahnhofstrasse, quite close to their hotel, and there is what claims to be an Old English tearoom upon the first floor. One goes up a wide flight of stairs with broad and shallow steps to a large room in the front with windows upon the street. The place is unaffectedly run for the benefit of visitors and particularly of English visitors, for there are English papers and periodicals there and the *décor* is that of Kensington in the early part of the century. A tendency to heavy gilt frames, bobble fringes, and moulded cornices and a complete absence of anything streamlined or chromium-plated combine to give an impression of permanence and solid comfort. Any Englishwoman suffering from homesickness for her native Bayswater would feel at home there at once. They even serve tea.

The result is that that room is indeed the resort of visitors; the Austrians do not frequent it. Why should they? Hambledon and Lombard met there upon the following morning after breakfast but too early for the assembly of persons desiring "elevenses," and sat in a corner to talk.

"I have one piece of news this morning," said Lombard. "You remember the old man who kept that antique shop in Innsbruck where Norz lived?"

"Grandpa Eisenschmidt? Perfectly."

"He has disappeared."

"In a sinister manner? Or merely rushed off somewhere to look at an alleged Vermeer?"

"Even I," said Lombard, "unsophisticated as I am, know that picture dealers hurriedly avert their eyes when anyone mentions Vermeer. No. He does—Eisenschmidt, I mean—quite often go away to visit sales or whatever dealers do when they go away, but his custom is to shut the shop and ask the police to keep an eye on it. This time the shop is shut, he has not informed the police, and his landlady says he has been gone two nights without telling her he was going away."

"That's funny," said Hambledon thoughtfully, "because, when I was leaning over a fence the other day, by the railway, thinking beautiful thoughts about Horaz, a train went by and I thought I saw the aged Eisenschmidt in it. But it was only a glimpse. I could easily have been mistaken."

"Going to or coming from Innsbruck?"

"Coming from."

"I will tell the police," said Lombard. "They can enquire at Scharnitz if they have not done so already. Speaking of Scharnitz, Horaz on his motorcycle did not cross the frontier yesterday."

"So he went somewhere this side of the frontier," said Hambledon. "Excuse my enunciation of the obvious; what I was really thinking was that if he is visiting a house along the road there somewhere, it is pleasantly within your own territory. I imagine you can have him watched and I hope it helps you to find your gang; it does not help me to find those infernal papers. What am I staying here for, Lombard? Apart from the pleasure of your company and the scenic delights of the Tyrol, the answer is an unpleasantly dry lemon. The gang think I've got them which

means that they haven't. I know I have not got them so it follows
that they are not here in Seefeld at all and I'm wasting my time.
I said to you yesterday that there was no reason to suppose that
Bastien ever brought those papers away from Calais, though he
apparently took them there. I shall leave this afternoon, Lombard,
get the night train from Basle to Calais—the same which Bastien
took—and have a look around there. Something might happen
to give me a lead."

"I will compose my mind to bid you a long farewell, for if
you are proposing to search Calais for a hidden packet small
enough to go flatly into a man's coat pocket——"

"Oh, not the town of Calais. Only the Maritime Station."

"Only. You said 'only'?"

"Now don't depress me," said Hambledon briskly. "The French
police, who are passionately interested since the design was stolen
—copied, then—in Paris, have gone into the matter thoroughly.
Bastien arrived at Calais at half past eleven in the morning and
stayed in the station until he left it at 18:40 by the Anglo-Swiss
to Basle. He had a leisurely lunch in the restaurant there, bought
some magazines at the bookstall, and sat or strolled about the
station all day. It is always crowded, the gang could hardly get
at him there and, in fact, the police noticed that he was never
very far from them all day. He was a well-known man; they
knew who he was. I expect he felt safe in the station but did
not dare to go out. As soon as the Basle train came into the
platform he took his place in it."

"But, my dear, good, optimistic friend," said Lombard pity-
ingly, "there must be millions of places in any station much
smaller than Calais Maritime where you could hide a small
packet and no one would ever find it——"

"I am not really quite so completely in the dark as a dead
black cat at the bottom of a well with a concrete cover cemented
down. I have the name of Albert."

"Who is Albert?"

"I have no idea. He may even be a town in France."

"Why," said Lombard with commendable patience, "Albert?"

"Bastien mentioned that name when he was dying; in fact, he
said it twice."

People were begining to drift in, women for the most part and nearly all English, to sink into the deep comfortable chairs and talk quietly over coffee. Many of them Hambledon recognized as guests at the Karwendelhof.

"I am not so much looking for the packet itself as for some indication of what he did with it," added Hambledon.

Colonel and Mrs. Grantham came in, waved to him, and sat down at the far end of the room.

"Such as someone having seen him climbing a ladder," said Lombard sarcastically, "to poke it away in the mechanism of the main-line signals? I will burn a candle for the success of your enterprise, my poor friend."

"I have now got three Governments urging me on," said Hambledon, "my own, France, and the United States. If I——"

The gawky lady Agatha Wiggins came in, paused to greet a number of friends—she appeared to know everybody including the proprietor—and saw Hambledon sitting in the corner. With a refined shriek of joy she swept towards him.

"Dear Mr. Hambledon! I have been looking for you, I have got something for you. Most curious and interesting. I will just run back to the hotel and fetch it. I am simply dying to know what it is."

"Please don't——" began Hambledon, but she was gone. "Lombard, have you met this lady? She will talk from now till doomsday."

"I have not met her in the accepted social sense, but I have observed her. If you do not wish to be pinned down to a long conversation, would it be a good idea to leave here and meet her in the road outside? You can stroll up towards the hotel. It is easier to get away, in the street."

"I would disappear altogether, but that would be so infernally rude. Why are we brought up to behave? It is very hampering. Yes, we will do as you say and then I will go to the hotel and pack. I wonder what she has got to show me?"

"A piece of edelweiss," suggested Lombard. "Yes, you go on to the hotel and I will follow you."

When they came out upon the street the first person they saw was Horaz, looking even more inane than usual and earning small tips by helping people to stow their luggage in one of the country buses which start their journeys from the Tourist Office almost next door. Beyond him, advancing with long strides, was the eager figure of Agatha Wiggins waving a handful of flimsy papers.

Hambledon gasped audibly and then hurried past Horaz to meet her as far from him as possible. If Hambledon thought that the meeting would be out of earshot from Horaz he was wrong, for Miss Wiggins had a carrying voice and she was excited.

"Look at these! I found them tucked away in that book you lent me, in the folded plans of the *Royal Albert*. But they do not look to me to be anything whatever to do with a ship; besides, they are in French, all the notes, I mean, and down here at the bottom it says something about a guided missile. I wonder how they got there? Isn't it exciting?"

Hambledon took the papers, folded them up, put them into an inside pocket, and buttoned his coat over them almost in one movement, babbling gratitude and apology all mixed up; he must simply rush, there was a telephone call from London for him at the hotel, he would tell her all about her find presently when he had had time to look at it. He beamed upon her with quite genuine delight, dodged round her, and hurried up the street with Lombard at his elbow.

"Horaz?" said Hambledon.

"His eyes nearly fell out," said Lombard. "He dropped somebody's parcel with a crashing sound as of china and rushed into the post office."

"He is telephoning," said Tommy, "and we are leaving. At least, I am."

"I'm coming with you until you can get some other form of protection."

"Good man."

They took a short cut through the main dining room and galloped up the stairs. Hambledon told Lombard in short bursts about the book which had been Bastien's.

"*How to Make Old-Time Ship Models*. I never gave the damn book another thought. Fool that I am! But he just had it lying about. It was on that little shelf affair when he was killed. I didn't even pick it up, the police shoved it into my rucksack. I never opened it. The *Royal Albert!*"

They entered Hambledon's room and he began hurling things into his rucksack.

"Which way did you think of going?" asked Lombard.

"Which way will they expect me to go?"

"To Innsbruck I assume, by road or train."

"Then I'll go the other way, into Germany at Scharnitz and get a train from Munich."

"I'll drive you to Munich," said Lombard. "I'll get a few things together and come back here for you. Hambledon, draw the curtains, lock the door after me, and—have you got a gun?"

"Yes."

"Sit facing the door. When I come back I will knock like this." Lombard tapped out a three-two-one rhythm. "If anybody else tries to get in, let them have it through the panels of the door."

Hambledon laughed suddenly and Lombard paused at the door long enough to ask what the joke was.

"Just wondering what Wilberger would say if I did. Our proprietor."

"Have you shot," said Lombard. "Justifiably." He went out and Tommy locked the door after him. However, no one came to the door before Lombard returned carrying another rucksack.

"My own few things," explained Lombard, "and a few groceries."

"Groceries. Groceries?"

"Things to eat. If we get really on the run we don't want to starve as well."

"Have you brought a tin opener?" asked Hambledon.

Lombard had left his car in the Bahnhofstrasse on the side opposite the hotel; there are gardens there with iron railings. The two men threw their rucksacks into the back of the car. Lombard got in, switched on and pressed the starter-button. The starter buzzed eagerly but the engine would not fire. Lombard tried again and again with the same result; he got out, opened the bonnet and looked inside.

"I suppose," said Tommy diffidently, "you've turned on the petrol?"

"I didn't turn it off."

"And—while on the subject—is she filled up?"

"Not enough for the whole journey," said Lombard, poking

rather aimlessly at the car's intestines, "but we can fill up at Scharnitz. I am not a motor mechanic."

"Nor I. Would it perhaps be better to consult one who is?"

"I'll go and get a man from the garage," said Lombard. With the unexpected agility so many fat men possess, he ran down the street and round the corner towards the garage. Something rustled behind the bushes; Hambledon, trying to peer through inadequate gaps, caught an imperfect glimpse of someone going away who might, conceivably, have been Horaz.

"You've got Horaz on the brain," said Tommy to himself. "Much more likely to have been the gardener. Still——"

He walked along to the Karwendelhof's forecourt, looked over the three or four cars which were parked there, and strolled thoughtfully back to Lombard's car. A few minutes later the owner returned almost literally towing a garage mechanic.

"I have a most important appointment," urged Lombard, "and I am already late. She was running all right this morning."

The garage man smiled patiently, flooded the carburettor, looked over the plug leads, got into the car and tried the starter. The same thing happened.

"It is a fine, warm day," he remarked. "It would seem that she wishes to make it a holiday. We will try to make her change her mind, *nicht wahr?*"

He switched off the engine, took off the distributor head, and broke into a laugh.

"The Herr's friends have been playing a joke on him." He poked a stubby finger at an empty cavity in the middle. "They have removed the rotor arm."

"Now what?" said Lombard.

"I may have another for this engine. I will go and see."

He closed the bonnet and walked casually away down the street, leaving a stricken silence behind him.

"Quick workers, these people," said Tommy, and began clearing their things out of the car in frantic haste. "Come on. I thought this might be so and I have anticipated the event. I have borrowed a car. Come on."

He led the rush to the Karwendelhof's forecourt, opened the door of a very smart Porsche sports car, threw his rucksack in, and got into the driving seat while Lombard leapt in on the other side.

"This is Walter's car," he said. "The man who runs the bar in the *Keller*. It's very good of him to lend it."

"Just so," said Hambledon, backing out carefully. "Nice fellow, Walter."

CHAPTER XIII

Frontier Post

The car shot down the street, turned right for Scharnitz, and then had to wait while the narrow stretch between the Tyroler Hof and the side of the clockmaker's house disencumbered itself of an oxcart closely followed by a big touring coach. There was also a group of visitors standing in the road to look in at the clockmaker's side window, for here there is no pavement.

"I feel eyes," said Hambledon, moving the gear-lever into first, "boring hot little holes in the back of my neck."

"I do not see Horaz," said Lombard, turning to look behind them.

"It may not be Horaz. You said the gang was a big one. He may have half-a-dozen little playmates in Seefeld."

"You are right, of course." The road cleared and Hambledon drove on. "Would you mind calling in at the police station along here before we——"

"I'm afraid I should," said Hambledon, and put his foot down.

"I want to give orders for Horaz's arrest——"

"I'm afraid Horaz will have to wait. I don't want to be over-taken by Walter. I thought I saw his face at the *Keller* window as we drove off."

"But he lent us——"

"He did indeed, but I fear I did not consult him first. Look in door-pockets and cubbyholes, Lombard, and see if the car's papers are in the car."

Lombard sighed. "If the gang don't get us, the police will."

"Don't fuss, Lombard. I wish you would hunt for the car's papers."

The Porsche is a very fast car and Hambledon was in a hurry; they were through Giessenbach before Lombard could announce that the papers were definitely not there. "I expect he carries them upon his person, we generally do." He put his hand in his pocket.

"You don't at the moment," said Hambledon, and spared a hand to toss them into his lap. "You left them on the seat of your car so I collected them. I thought they might come in handy."

"I must have been excited," said Lombard apologetically. "But these will not——"

"They will do to wave at people to allay their suspicions till I can crash the barrier," said Tommy calmly, and Lombard looked at him with something like horror. "You know, added Hambledon, "I have never been a policeman."

"I believe that," said Lombard emphatically, "without a moment's hesitation."

"The training," pursued Hambledon, "excellent as it is, tends to cramp initiative. Another thing we might do is to have not only our passports at the ready but our official cards with them. We might with luck get through on those if we are stopped."

Lombard agreed enthusiastically. "I am glad to hear that you are prepared to employ legal methods if only as a last resort." He took out his official card, slipped it inside his passport, and put both in the door-pocket of the car to be immediately at hand.

"There's Scharnitz ahead," said Hambledon. "Where exactly is this frontier post?"

"Through the town and a little way past the station. It is a short distance outside the town."

Hambledon slowed down for the narrow streets.

"Can one see the frontier post from afar off, or does one come upon it suddenly round a corner?"

"There is a curve. As we are going, a right-hand curve with a high wall. There is a slight up gradient. On the left——"

"Can you stop me just before I come into view of the post?"

"Certainly," said Lombard. "But——"

"I will stop as I said, just out of sight of the frontier post, and you will please get out and walk on to a point where you can see both the post and me. We will wait until something slow and heavy comes along, a timber-tug loaded with tree trunks would be ideal. He will stop, go in to have his papers stamped, exchange a little hearty backchat with the frontier police, and climb slowly back into his vehicle. At that moment you take your handkerchief from your pocket as a signal and I will move forward, you will leap aboard with your customary rubber-ball-like agility, which always astonishes me, and we will dash past him and under the barrier while it is raised to let him pass. There's the station, it can't be far now."

"It isn't."

"Is that all clear?"

"Quite. Do you choose which vehicle to follow?"

"I do," said Tommy Hambledon. "I will make a long nose at it to indicate the object of my choice."

"Why do you not pull up short of the post but within sight so that you may choose for yourself the exact moment to advance?"

"Because, my dear innocent warrior, though I don't believe for a moment that Walter would report us to the police or that Wilberger would let him if he wanted to, Horaz may have done so. 'Achtung! Achtung! Is this the frontier post? A villain has stolen my beautiful cream-coloured Porsche, number so-and-so.' Then they shut the barriers as soon as they——"

"Stop here," said Lombard. Hambledon pulled in close to the right-hand wall and Lombard sprang out, crossed the road, and walked on about twenty yards to a point where he could see the red-and-white striped poles and the customs and frontier officials walking about them. Hambledon got out his own passport, put his official card into it, and looked up in surprise as Lombard came hurrying back.

"Very odd. The men are all in plain clothes. It almost looks as if something unusual had happened."

"It would appear so," said Hambledon, and his Lüger came

out of his pocket to lie on his knees. "Get back to your place, this fellow might do."

"This fellow" was a large ancient saloon car of German make loaded down with luggage on the roof as well as on the grid. It seemed to be well filled with passengers and was being inexpertly driven by a very young man, his face bright scarlet with effort and embarrassment, who was being instructed by an elderly man sitting next him. As they passed, the young driver bungled, with gnashing sounds, his gear-change, looked down to see what he was doing and almost rammed the wall. A few educational acidities floated back to Hambledon's ears; the car swerved suddenly and drove on. He made the prearranged rude gesture for Lombard's benefit and was rewarded by the sight of a very young face at the back window with its tongue sticking out in reply.

"I suppose," said Tommy to himself, "it's too much to hope that you'll stamp on the accelerator instead of the brake and 'open up dem pearly gates for me' like a charging buffalo? More likely to block them up altogether. You want jam on it," he reproached himself, putting the car into gear ready to make a quick start. There is always a certain delay while someone from the car walks across to the office to get his papers stamped, but there seemed to be some disorganization this morning. Frontier guards in plain clothes are a thought at which the well-trained mind boggles.

Lombard's handkerchief came out; as Hambledon went forward he came running to leap in at the door which Tommy had opened for him.

"The owner did not get out—the man took the papers and——"

As the car topped the rise and the barrier came into view, it could be seen that one of them was rising hesitantly and the ancient saloon was not yet moving. Hambledon lifted his foot momentarily, but the old car lumbered forward and the barrier rose at last. There were only two men ostensibly on duty and both were watching the saloon.

Hambledon changed into third and put his foot hard down. The murmur of the engine rose to a snarl and one of the men in mufti looked round to see the cream-coloured Porsche only thirty yards off and leaping at him. He uttered a loud yell and brought the barrier down again smartly, right across the luggage-encumbered roof of the old saloon. The Porsche is a long, low car and the speedometer needle was rising fast.

"That man on the left is one of the gang," said Lombard calmly and drew his revolver from his pocket, but the alleged frontier guard had his already in his hand and fired several shots at close range at the Porsche as it roared past him. As the car shot under the barrier Hambledon ducked down upon the driving wheel but Lombard slid down in his seat, threw his head back and saw the red-and-white pole pass over a foot above his head.

"Car on the right probably theirs," said Hambledon, "can you hit it?"

Lombard whirled round, gun in hand, and fired five shots into the front of a green Mercedes which was standing at the side of the road with its engine running. At the same instant a fusillade of shots broke out from the barrier and the driving mirror beside Hambledon shattered into fragments.

"They have dared to capture the frontier post," said Lombard in a scandalized voice.

"Did you hit the car?"

"Oh, yes. I don't know what damage I did, they are running round it," said Lombard, looking back. "They don't seem—we are out of sight."

"Man on the right," said Hambledon suddenly, and his Lüger was in his hand. "Hold her straight, I'll——"

But the man, who had risen from behind a bush with a tommy gun in his hand, fired a burst at the front tyres. There was a loud bang as one of them burst, and the car swerved violently across the road out of control. Hambledon yelled to Lombard to jump for it as the Porsche hit the grass verge, turned end for end, rolled into the bushes, and burst into flames.

Hambledon's progress was stopped by some bushes; he was mildly surprised to find himself not merely alive but still clutching his automatic. He wriggled round to face the road and saw the man with the tommy gun walking towards them. No doubt it must have seemed that there was nothing to fear from participants in a crash like that. He was quite young and looked a little alarmed and even apologetic, like a small boy who has fired an air gun at a cat and winged the vicar.

Hambledon waited till he was only ten paces away and shot him dead.

From the point of view of someone's trying to track someone else, there is much to be said for the Tyrol—from many other points of view also, of course—but Medeski was a man of one idea, to regain those papers, and he kept his mind tightly to his task. The advantage of hunting anyone in the Tyrol lies in the fact that it is mainly composed of precipitous mountains divided by narrow steep-walled valleys through which the roads run and must run. There are of course walkers' tracks over the hills, but they are not even suitable for walkers, unless they are active, and certainly not for motorcycles. Once, therefore, a motorcyclist was clear of the streets of Seefeld on the Scharnitz road, he could confidently be looked for at successive points upon that road; if he failed to pass any one of them it meant that he had left the road before that point *on foot*. Presumably he would hide his machine behind bushes. Medeski, poring over his *Wanderkarte* in his clean, bare little bedroom, came correctly to this conclusion.

Moreover, there were not so many places where Eugene would leave the road. He would not, for example, cross the river where there was no bridge, nor where he would immediately be faced with unclimbable rock faces. If this place was one to which men habitually resorted, it must be reasonably easy of access. Medeski walked to Scharnitz along the road. There is a turning into the woods just before Giessenbach and here he sat down for a rest. He was rewarded by the sight of Eugene roaring past the turn without so much as a passing glance. Not there, not there, my child, not there. Medeski walked on.

He spent a couple of days making enquiries at roadside cafés about a friend whom he was to have met and in laying out a little money here and there as a reward for information, until the point of Eugene's departure from the road was narrowed down to a short stretch between the far side of Scharnitz village and the frontier. Here there was a walkers' track leading up to the Arn Spitze. Eugene usually went out in the afternoon; very well, Medeski would go up there in the morning. His kind landlady provided him with a packed lunch before he set off by train to Scharnitz.

He kept to the right side of the Bahnhofstrasse going up to Seefeld station because on the other side, where the shops are, he saw from afar the gangling figure of Eugene-as-Horaz loading luggage into a bus outside the Tourist Bureau. Medeski walked steadily by upon the opposite footpath and did no more than glance across when a gawky woman came down from the Karwendelhof Hotel waving some sheets of paper in her hand and talking loudly, presumably about them, in a voice like a peahen, to a man who was coming up to meet her. Her words were perfectly audible to Medeski but, alas, he did not understand English.

When he arrived at Scharnitz station he turned right, away from the town, and was immediately encouraged by the sight of a group of obviously serious walkers ahead of him; they carried stout sticks, wore sturdy boots, and strode out purposefully. One of them even had a coil of rope slung round him. They led the way across a bridge over the river. Medeski, not actually joining the party, trailed after them as they entered the woods, and the path began to climb. After a time he lost sight of them; they walked faster than he and, besides, he was delayed by looking for feasible turnings off the path. He investigated several places which looked possible but they all petered out and he plodded on again.

He had been walking for an hour or more and had passed the rest hut at the head of the Hasel Lahne when he heard steps and voices behind him of men not yet in sight. The voices were speaking German and, though what they said did not tell him anything definite—they were too guarded for that—it was clear that they had played some trick on somebody and were delighted about it. Not innocent delight, such as one might expect from harmless tourists, but with a suggestion of savagery about it.

Medeski left the path hurriedly and went to ground like a rabbit.

There were four men together, each of them carrying a bulging rucksack. They kept close together and the voice of the first was the voice of Eugene.

Medeski waited until they had gone by out of sight and then followed on. He went past the point where they had turned off because he heard voices ahead which he took for theirs; it was not until he came to the stretch where the real rock climbing begins and one helps oneself up by a fixed wire rope that he realized that the voices he was hearing were those of the original walking party from Scharnitz coming back. He sat down upon a rock, opened his parcel of lunch, and waited for them. When they came down they saw a tidy little man—Medeski was constitutionally tidy—sitting at the side of the track eating buttered rolls and hard-boiled egg. They looked at him, at his shoes, at each other, and stopped.

"Excuse me, I beg," said one of them in a particularly pleasant voice. "I hope the Herr will not think me rudely intrusive, but is the Herr thinking of going on to the top by himself?"

"I thank the Herr," said Medeski, "but no. I think I have walked far enough."

"Not wishing to interfere with the Herr's pleasures for a moment," went on the stranger, "but it is really not very safe up there for one man alone unless he is an experienced mountaineer."

"Is there, then," asked Medeski, "no one else further up the hill?"

"No one," said another of the party, with a laugh. "We had the whole mountaintop entirely to ourselves."

"And you met no one, as you were coming down?"

"No one at all. So, forgive me, you will not venture further?"

"Oh, no," said Medeski truthfully. "I have come far enough. I shall but finish my lunch, have a little rest, and walk down again. I thank the Herren most sincerely for their kindly interest."

"Not at all," they said, and wished him a pleasant afternoon. When they had started again Medeski watched them out of sight.

"Most helpful," he murmured to himself, "most. They met no one; therefore I have passed the turn. I shall not miss it when I go back."

CHAPTER XIV

The Arn Spitze

The Austrian Frontier Post at Scharnitz appeared to have gone out of action. Cars came up on both sides and stopped, two or three abreast, while others came up behind; their owners, surprised to see no police on duty, got out with flapping papers in their hands and wandered into the offices on either side. Here also were no clerks on duty; the rubber stamps lay idle, the ruled and columned registers stared blankly at the ceiling. Notices and lists of dutiable articles, tacked with drawing-pins to the walls, rustled drily in the intermittent breeze while the travellers banged vainly upon the counters and uttered the equivalent of "Hi!" in at least six languages. Outside, at the rear of the accumulation on either side, impatient cars began to sound their horns.

One of the waiting crowd was an Englishman, unmistakeable in tweeds; another an American Army officer in uniform. They glanced at each other, their eyes met, and they moved towards each other, for upon such occasions as this the English-Speaking Union is not limited to membership of an organization but operates automatically.

"Surely," said the Englishman, "this is a little unusual? There is generally someone about in these places."

"Yes, sir," said the American. "I come this way, sir, quite a lot and this is the first time I have found it unattended."

"I find it hard to believe that they would all go to lunch simultaneously," said the Englishman. "Especially without their hats."

"Without their hats?" The American followed the Englishman's glance towards a table at the back of the office where five uniform hats lay together. "And their keys!

"You are right." The Englishman listened and shook his head. "I thought I heard a banging noise somewhere but I can't be sure with all this babble going on."

"Soon stop that." The American lifted his voice and spoke authoritatively in German. "Silence, please, for a moment. Quiet, please."

One or two people looked at him indignantly for, indeed, this was not even the American Zone of Occupation, but there was a hush in which could faintly be heard the sound as of a door being kicked and a voice shouting something.

"Sounds like somebody's gotten himself locked in," said the American with a slow smile. "Sir, shall we make a two-man rescue party?"

"I'm with you," said the Englishman. "Lead on."

They passed the counter, picked up the keys, and went on through a doorway at the back. From here it was possible plainly to hear cries of wrath with bumps and bangs.

"I've never been inside a frontier post before," said the Englishman in a pleased voice. "No further than the counter, I mean. Do they keep cells here for awkward customers, do you know?"

"I wouldn't know from personal experiences," said the American, "but I would say that some such facilities would just naturally be provided. Seems like it's along here."

It was easy to identify the door which contained those anxious to be let out; after some fumbling with the wrong keys it opened and frontier police and customs officials rushed out and along the passage into the office. Their rescuers offered each other cigarettes and strolled placidly after them. When they in their turn reached the office, one of the customs men was frantically jiggling the telephone and shouting into it. He suddenly replaced the receiver and announced dramatically that the wires had been cut.

"So excitable, these foreigners," murmured the Englishman and the American looked at him.

"Well, wouldn't you say they'd had something to get excited

about? What is it all about, anyway? Hey, you!" He grabbed a passing official by the arm and brought him up standing. "What's going on around here, anyway?"

"It is a gang of smugglers who seized the post and locked us all up. They said that they were running a big lorry through with contraband and if we did not see it we could not describe it. They said it would not be for long and they would leave the keys. Excuse me." He freed himself and hurried away.

"I wonder whether they captured the German one, too," said the Englishman.

"It was perfectly O.K. when I came through, perfectly O.K. I didn't meet any big lorry, either. There was a crashed car burning but there were people round it. I didn't stop."

Hambledon wasted no time upon the late owner of the tommy gun. He had fallen on the edge of the grass and looked at a glance like a casualty of the car crash. Tommy staggered to his feet and was relieved to see advancing, gigantic through the smoke from the blazing car, the rotund form of Lombard. He was still carrying his revolver in one hand; with the other he was mopping with his handkerchief a long ugly tear down one cheek but he seemed otherwise undamaged. Hambledon seized him by the arm.

"Quick, let's get away before the gang turn up. Down into the smoke there and across the river. We'll take to the woods."

Fortunately for them the smoke was blowing down and rolling across the narrow stretch of meadow between the road and the river. Half-blinded but happily aware that any pursuers would be even more blinded, they pounded down the slope, struggled thigh-deep through the water of the Isar, and took to the woods. Almost at once the land started to rise steeply and Lombard led the way up between the trees at a pace which alarmed Hambledon; he had not yet acquired the faculty of bounding up mountain sides at high altitudes without getting painfully blown.

"I suppose," he gasped, "you've been doing this sort of thing ever since you learned to walk."

"Yes. You'll get used to it. Come on."

They went on until Hambledon's pumping lungs demanded a halt, though he noticed with almost painful envy that Lombard was not even breathing faster than usual. They paused to look back through a gap in the trees at the valley far below them blotched by an ugly patch of black smoke with flames leaping out of it. Hambledon made a great effort to control his breathing and managed to draw one long breath and then another.

"It looks," he said, "as though the British Government will have to buy Walter another Porsche."

"Quiet," said Lombard in a low tone. "Listen."

Hambledon could hear nothing plainly for the blood still thumping in his ears, but Lombard was listening intently. Presently he moved abruptly.

"They're after us," he murmured. "I thought they would be. Come on now and try not to make a noise."

He turned and went on with the mountaineer's long stride which looks slow but is not; Hambledon, who had got his second wind, strode after him. He was annoyed with himself; he had always been of a spare figure, not running to fat, and had kept himself in good condition; yet here he was being run to a standstill by a man with three double chins and a figure like Monsieur Bibendum, the Michelin Tyre advertisement. Humiliating. Hambledon's jaw came forward and he kept up. Fortunately Lombard was no longer climbing straight up; he was more or less following a contour line and though the going was desperately rough, Hambledon found it manageable.

Presently Lombard, who had taken to zigzagging without apparent reason, stopped and spoke in a low tone.

"Quiet. Keep close to me. Do as I do."

He slipped round a clump of bushes and went down on his knees to crawl forward upon a sort of rock shelf; when he came out upon this he went down flat and crept forward upon his elbows. When Hambledon joined him Lombard said, "Keep your head down. Right down. Peep through the stems as I do."

The stems were those of some wiry plants not more than a foot high. Hambledon parted them with his fingers—"Do not agitate them!"—and peered cautiously between.

They were upon the extreme edge of an outcrop of rock which dropped away sheer for thirty feet below them. Just to their right a short section of a track was visible below and there a man was standing, looking about him and listening. After a few minutes he moved on up the path and out of sight.

Lombard edged nearer Hambledon and spoke with his mouth close to his ear.

"That open patch down there more to the left. In line with that culvert under the railway. There's another man there."

There was, though Hambledon did not pick him up until he moved. He was not looking towards them but away to his left; when he saw what he was looking for he waved his arm, turned to come on up the hill, and disappeared from sight.

"Three," said Tommy.

"Four," corrected Lombard. "There's a man in a peaked cap I saw earlier, not one of these. Come on."

They wriggled backwards off their shelf, crawled round their clump of bushes and rose to their feet. There followed half an hour or more of such violent exertion as Hambledon had not undergone since he was a very young man, and even then he was not running for his life. In one short pause Lombard deigned to explain that the men were trying to drive them up against the rock faces of the Arn Spitze where they would stand a rather poor chance. "Two of them had rifles," said Lombard. "Did you notice? I wish I had mine."

"Where is yours?" asked Hambledon idly.

"In my car at Seefeld. Come on."

They rounded a curve of the hillside, still among trees, and came upon a small but active mountain stream which Lombard apparently considered a nice path in which to walk. It was not, it was excessively rough; once when Tommy slipped off a rock and set a small patch of moraine sliding, Lombard addressed him in a manner he had not heard since he was a small boy. Before he could think of, or gather breath for, an adequate reply, they went up a waterfall which resisted their advances with malign energy. They reached the top at last, wrung some of the water out of their trousers, and set off at a lumbering trot along a sort of terrace which was, for once, almost reasonably smooth. On their left was a rock face; the kind of thing, Hambledon reflected, which it was better not to be driven up against, but presumably Lombard knew where he was going. The shelf nar-

rowed to a ledge round an outcrop of rock. Lombard dropped
to a walk to go round it and stopped so suddenly that Hambledon
cannoned into him from behind and nearly went over the edge.

Within six feet of them three men were standing together and
they wore the uniform of the German frontier guards.

The corporal in charge stared for a moment, saluted and said,
"Good afternoon, gentlemen."

"You startled me," said Lombard with a laugh. "One does not
often meet people up here."

"Walkers up here," agreed the German, "usually keep to the
path, though doubtless real mountaineers like the Herren prefer
to make their own way." His glance fell to the shoes they were
both wearing; experienced mountaineers wear nailed boots.

"We are not really climbing," said Lombard casually. "We are
just putting in a little practice after being too long away from
the hills."

"I understand," said the German. "We also, with other patrols,
are here only because it seems there has been a little trouble at
the frontier. May I ask if the Herren were involved in it at all?"

"Dear me, no," said Hambledon before Lombard could answer.
"At the frontier post? We did not cross the frontier, we turned
off in Scharnitz."

"Nevertheless, you did cross the frontier somewhere, for the
Herren are now in Germany," said the man with a pleasant
smile. "May I see your passports, please?"

Lombard said steadily, "I am sorry, I have not mine with me.
I left it behind." Hambledon, who had put his hand inside his
coat and found nothing, suddenly remembered.

"I am a fool! I left it on the seat of the bus—you remember
Lucius? We got out in rather a hurry; we expected to be going
on a little further."

"May I, then, have the Herren's names?"

"Lucius Lombard, of the Austrian Special Police."

"Oh, indeed?" said the German, with lively interest. "I have
heard, naturally, of the Herr Lombard. This does not, however,
as the Herr will be the first to admit, excuse me from the duty
of making certain of the Herr's identity."

"Of course not——"

"Your official card?"

"This is not my lucky day," said Lombard. "I have not that, either." He laughed easily, but the corporal did not appear to be amused. He turned to Hambledon.

"And the Herr's name is——"

"Thomas Elphinstone Hambledon, British subject. I live in London," said Tommy, and gave his full address. "At the moment I am staying at the Karwendelhof at Seefeld."

"The Herr is on holiday?" said the corporal, making notes in his little book.

"That is so, yes."

The German closed his book and proceeded to explain to Lombard, with an equal mixture of politeness and determination, the unavoidable necessity for their accompanying him to the German Frontier Post so that their identities could be checked. "For I have not the honour of knowing the Herr personally. I regret the inconvenience."

"No inconvenience," said Lombard cheerfully. "My own fault, entirely. I expect——"

"*Hands up!*"

The corporal spun round. Behind him, at a turn in the path, there stood four men, all with firearms in their hands. Wise men, taken by surprise, obey such orders backed by such menaces; the Germans, who were neither fools nor bent upon suicide, obeyed promptly. Hambledon and Lombard did the same.

"Line them up," said the leader. "Not close together, space them out." He was a tall slim man with an incisive manner of speech. "That is right. Erich, you and Marc disarm them. Paulus, take the weapons from them and throw them over the edge here. Be quick. I do not advise you gentlemen to resist, for I will shoot at once any man who puts down his hands."

The work was soon done.

"Seems a p-pity," said Paulus, hurling finally Hambledon's Lüger into the treetops below, "to throw away all these good guns. They m-might b-be useful to us."

"Is that all?" asked the leader. "No knives, even? Good. Now then, gentlemen. Your clothes, please. Be quick."

"Clothes?" said the corporal. "You want our uniforms I suppose."

"I want every stitch you have on you down to your socks and boots."

"But," said the corporal, glaring at him, "this is unseemingly."

"Get on with it!"

"But——"

The leader lowered the automatic pistol till it pointed at the corporal's feet and fired. The German leapt in the air and the bullet went into the ground.

"On your way down to your post," said the man called Erich in a thick slow voice, "perhaps you may find growing some fig leaves by the roadside." He grinned.

"Or thistles," said Paulus, a man so fair as to be almost an albino. "Thistle. M-much m-more suitable."

Hambledon undressed quite automatically, hardly aware of what he was doing because his mind was back at Basle in the flat which had been Bastien's, listening with Cournand and Virolet to a tape recording of a conversation over dinner when three men planned to steal designs and money from a renegade Frenchman and a Russian. Eugene, Erich, and Paulus Caron, the same men with the same voices. Of course he and Lombard had been perfectly right in assuming that Horaz was Eugene in disguise, the man must be a superb actor. He did not, now, look in the least like a village idiot though—the sun slanting through the trees dazzled Hambledon's eyes and he moved slightly—though Horaz-Eugene still had the remains of a very choice black eye.

"Marc," said Eugene, "go and get the rucksacks."

The man went without a word but Paulus asked, "What for?"

"To put these clothes in, of course. You do not propose to walk these hills with garments hanging over your arm like a shop-walker, do you?"

Paulus giggled but Erich who should, Hambledon had thought at Basle, have been nicknamed "Little by Little, for such were his mental processes, had another suggestion.

"Why not go through the things here, for then we should not have to carry them at all?"

"For several reasons," said Eugene. "One, because it would be unwise to loiter here; the sooner we get out of sight the better. Two, because it will be more convenient; we can do the job more thoroughly at leisure. Three, because it amuses me to think of these pompous busybodies limping home in bare feet clothed only in blushes. Four, because I say so and that's enough."

At this point Marc returned with four almost empty rucksacks dangling from one shoulder. He rounded the corner, came suddenly upon the scene, stopped abruptly and doubled up with laughter.

"He is quite right," said Eugene. "I wish I had a mirror to show you how absurd you look. The two young constables might pass if one were not too particular and the Englishman is not too bad for a man of his age, but corporal, your stomach! As for the important and distinguished Herr Lombard, the sight of him really shocks me. Quite obscene——Pack those things, men, don't stand staring. Perhaps it is blowing mouth organs which has inflated the Herr so regrettably. Do they perhaps lose patience and blow back——Yes, Erich, what is it?"

"Do we really need the constables' clothes as well? Why?"

"Because," said Eugene between his teeth, "whichever of those two was carrying those papers will have passed them to the police for safe carriage. I myself would have passed them to that pink-faced blue-eyed new recruit on the left in the hope that mugs like you would think exactly what you are thinking. All done? Good, now we go."

He swung one of the rucksacks upon his back; the other three men did the same. One by one they sidled carefully round the spur of rock by the way Hambledon and Lombard had come and one by one, grinning widely as they went, they disappeared from sight.

CHAPTER XV

What Time Is It?

It is natural for a group of men involved in difficulty to look at each other. This group did not.

"This," said the corporal bitterly, "is most unseemly." His two constables growled.

"You said that before," said Lombard, "and it is even more true now it has happened."

"Horribly true," said Hambledon briskly, "and what are we going to do about it?"

"We are going to walk down to the post," said the corporal, "and you two gentlemen are coming with us, as I said before we were interrupted."

"The post is on the road," said the younger constable gloomily, "in full view of the passers-by. How are we to approach it once we are within view?"

"We will form ourselves into a tight ring, facing inwards," said Hambledon, "and revolve remorselessly towards it."

Lombard glanced at him and noticed that Tommy was having difficulty in keeping the corners of his mouth steady; his own twitched in sympathy.

"We will deal with that when we come to it," said the corporal sensibly. *"Vorwärts!"*

They started. They were upon a path of sorts but it was for

the most part stony and unkind to bare feet. Hambledon and
Lombard, picking their way, managed well enough, and the two
young constables, with an occasional stumble and curse, made
steady headway, but the corporal, who was middle-aged and
heavy in build, was very soon distressed and their progress was
slowed to a crawl.

"It is my feet," he complained. "I always had tender feet even
as a child. These stones—*ach!*"

"At this rate," said Tommy in Lombard's ear, "the gang will
be to hell and gone with those papers before ever we reach that
damned post. And what good will it do us when we do reach it?"

"What else can we do?"

"Run for it and see where they go."

"Those two young men will catch us."

"I shall risk it in a minute," said Hambledon. "This is driving
me——"

The corporal slipped, uttered a strangled yelp, and fell heavily.
His men sprang to his side but when he sat up it could be seen
that his right foot was bleeding badly where he had cut it upon
a stone.

"And not even a rag to tie round it!" he stormed. "When I
catch those devils——Men, you must carry me. I can help myself
along with the other foot."

The constables heaved him up between them, supported his
weight upon his arms round their necks, and gripped him round
the waist. When the group of three was nearly as inextricably
involved as the Laocoön, Hambledon touched Lombard's arm
and said, "Now." They turned and ran back up the path.

Since bare feet make little noise, the police did not at once
notice that they had gone. By the time one of the constables
glanced over his shoulder they were thirty yards away and
going strong."

"The prisoners are escaping!" he said, and made to disentangle
himself, but the corporal only tightened his grip.

"Let them," he said. "They will not get far like that. Our first
duty is to report. That gang also—they are, as it were, upon an
island surrounded by roads which must be patrolled. They cannot eventually escape."

The group closed up again and doggedly went its way.

"We must be careful," said Lombard to Hambledon. "We are horribly conspicuous."

"We will find a patch of bog and roll in it. Press on, press on. 'Duty before decency, Mr. Easy.'"

"We can, perhaps, do better than that, just a moment—yes. Over this ridge and down a little, there is one of those little huts for hay; there might be some sacks in it."

Lombard turned left through the trees and there followed a sliding scramble downhill till they came out upon a tiny meadow where the flowering grasses were up to their thighs; in the middle was the small wooden shack of which the Austrian had spoken.

"One has to walk through the hay to get to it," said Hambledon. "Why don't they put these huts at the edge?"

"Never do that," said Lombard, striding ahead. "If the hay were damp and the hut flared up, what about the trees? Dreadful things, forest fires."

The door was open and they went in. As Lombard had had reason to expect, there were a couple of sacks there, old and thin but large and beautifully dim in colour. Lombard pounced on them.

"Only two? One each. I had hoped——"

"Quick," said Hambledon. "A slit for the head and one for each arm, and we're dressed. Will they tear? Will they—hell! A piece of broken glass——"

"Here's a bottle," said Lombard, and broke it. A minute or so filled with small tearing noises provided them with a garment which almost reached their knees and was even wide enough to surround Lucius Lombard though Hambledon's flapped loosely upon him.

"I wish there had been just one more," said Tommy. "It would be a good idea to bind up our feet, mine are wearing a bit thin in places already—here's something." A grubby lump on the floor was yet another sack so torn that it had been discarded and thrown down; slit into strips it served to bandage their feet after a fashion and even provided enough stringlike ravel for Hambledon to tie round his waist.

"Dressy, are you not?" said Lombard, watching this.

"My shirt's too big for me, I fall about in it. Now where's some nice brown mud? I say, this is better. Wonderful prop for morale, a nice large sack."

They returned to the cover of the trees, and the first tiny rill they came to ran into a little basin rimmed round with peaty mud which they scooped up with their hands and rubbed over themselves, faces and hair included.

"My goodness," said Hambledon, "that's the best camouflage I've ever seen. If you stood against a tree trunk and didn't move, a man wouldn't see you till he ran into you. Turn round, there's a white patch behind your shoulder. Am I all right? We look like what I believe are called Troglodytes, whatever they are. Come on. That is, if you have any idea where to make for."

"We will start by getting on the walkers' track to the Arn Spitze, this way. I am pretty sure the gang have a hideout somewhere about here; when I have followed suspects before, they have vanished in this area."

"Could they not go right over the ridge and down into the next valley? The Leutasch Valley, is it?"

"They could, being mountaineers, but it's a long way and quite tricky in places. Long before they could get there, there will be police patrols on foot, cycle, and motorcycle passing up and down all these roads looking out for them, our friends the frontier guards will see to that as soon as they reach a telephone."

"Looking for us, too?" asked Hambledon.

"Oh, I imagine so. The corporal didn't like us much, did he? Did you notice, he thought at first that the gang was a rescue party?"

"He must have changed his mind when they treated us all alike."

"And may have changed it again when we ran off to catch them up," said Lombard, "for that's what it must have looked like. By the way, did you also notice how Horaz-Eugene—we were quite right—spoke about examining the clothes 'thoroughly, at leisure'? Nobody would call galloping about on the Riedberg leisure, and somehow I got the idea that it wasn't far."

"I thought so, too. By the way, you mentioned Horaz-Eugene. I know who two of the others were, too, Erich and Paulus. I recognized their voices from that tape recorder at Basle I told you about."

"Oh, they were those same men, were they? When I heard Paulus's name I wondered."

"And another thing," said Hambledon. "That fellow I shot dead on the roadside after the Porsche crashed. I don't think the gang can have heard the sad news, do you? Otherwise surely they would have taken reprisals."

"I daresay he was told to make himself scarce and hide up till the excitement had died down. There might have been a car along at any moment. Well now, here is the Arn Spitze track."

"And we go up," said Hambledon, "for I think we have joined it lower down than they did, am I right? We are not so far from civilization here."

"Up, certainly. If I'm right about their hideout, it will be higher up where it is not safe for walkers to stray from the path, up there where the precipices are."

"I shall stray from the path like a startled cat if I see any walkers coming," said Hambledon energetically. "What a country yours is! Do you realize that this is the second time within a week that I've been stripped to the skin by your charming fellow countrymen?"

"It is really the only way," said Lombard mildly, "if one is to search clothing thoroughly. You must know that."

"Maybe, but for my next holiday I shall go to Blackpool!"

They walked on for a time in silence, up and up, with the bare rocks of the Arn Massif ever more nearly above them. The path zigzagged across the face of the hill, still among trees which here were one above another rather than side by side. At several places the path was soft and damp and Hambledon stopped to examine the surface.

"I wish I were a boy scout," he said, "and had learned all about footprints."

"There are a good many people up here from time to time, on fine days. Not troops of sightseers, but fairly frequent walkers as far as the shelter hut we passed just now. From now on, it is a climb. I am looking for——"

"Tell me," said Hambleton, still with his eyes on the ground, "is chewing coke a local vice?"

"Chewing coke?"

"Or do people carry bits of it as a mascot?"

"Certainly not. What on earth would people want with coke up here? There's plenty of wood."

"I don't know in the least, but somebody has been carrying coke here." Hambledon picked up what was certainly a small piece of coke though it was no bigger than his thumbnail. "That's the fourth piece I've seen. I picture a sack with a small hole in it and every now and again a tiny piece drops out. Look at it yourself."

Lombard took it. "Coke it is. Well now, that is odd. I suppose the gang would be the only people to want coke up here, you would not take it on a picnic! But what for? It is scarce and expensive in Austria and, as I said, there is all this wood. What I was going to say was that we must look out for a place where it would be possible to turn off and there are not so many, as you see. They will be very careful, too, not to leave a marked trail."

"There is a sort of ridge runs off to the left here."

"I know that of old. It is deceptive, it goes nowhere. You come to a waterfall you cannot pass because it runs in a deep gully, and on the further side there is only a precipice to face you. A sort of rib running down the mountainside."

"All the same," urged Hambledon, "let us go along there and look."

"It is of no use. No one who knows this mountain well would turn off there."

"I am sure you are right, but none the less I want just to walk a little way along it."

"I had better come with you, then," said Lombard patiently, "for it is quite easy to kill yourself along there."

Hambledon led the way along what was no more than a narrow shelf across the downward sweep of the mountain side. They went on perhaps thirty yards when suddenly he stooped to pick up something.

"Coke, again," he said in a low voice. "You know, this track is not too bad and it has been used lately. There are footmarks here."

"I have not been along here since I was a boy and lived at Scharnitz," said Lombard in the same cautious tone, "but it looks to me as though it had been improved."

They went on with great precaution since, owing to the trees and the curves of the mountainside they could seldom see more than a few yards ahead, until on rounding a corner they heard the sound of falling water not far away.

"Get down and crawl," whispered Lombard urgently. "They cannot cross that water; they may be all about us behind these rocks. We are mad, naked and unarmed——"

The next discovery was another soft patch and bootmarks. Hambledon pointed them out and crawled on. The waterfall came in sight suddenly when they were close upon it, a long wavering trail of water white as lace, falling from a height above into a pool below and obliterating all other sounds with its own steady roar.

Lombard caught Hambledon's arm and shook his head; Hambledon pointed at the rock wall on their side of the torrent and nodded. Lombard crept past him and looked down. There were points of rock projecting like almost impossible steps and upon two of them were the fresh marks of nailed boots.

Hambledon joined his hands in the gesture of one who engages in prayer, grinned at Lombard, and lowered himself down the rocks. It became plain at once that the hillside curved back here so that the water fell clear of the rock and there was space behind. More, there was a ledge, a wide one two or three feet wide, natural in origin but having been improved by the hand of man. It was wet and slimy but not dangerous to a man with a steady head. It tilted slightly inwards and upon its green-stained surface there were clear marks of frequent use.

Hambledon rose to his feet and walked steadily along it with Lombard close upon his heels. When they had passed the water, there was another steep bank on the further side with footholds cut in the rock and iron stanchions driven in for handholds. They went up quickly until, with immense caution, they could look over the top.

There was undergrowth to screen them and a path twisting through it to a quite large natural terrace. The cliff above overhung it; opposite to them the great projecting rib of which Lombard had spoken barred access from the further side; below the terrace the cliff fell away in sheer and naked rock a hundred feet and more to be lost in the trees below. In the face of the cliff backing the terrace there was a dark recess which might be the entrance to a cave; close to this a man sat upon a lump of rock with a bucket at his feet, prosaically peeling potatoes.

Hambledon and Lombard climbed down the bank, passed under the waterfall, climbed up the other side, and took again the narrow and tortuous trail among the trees. They did not speak and Lombard noticed that though Hambledon took every precaution before entering upon a fresh stretch of the way, he yet went as fast as possible between these points. As the path improved he was practically running.

"Careful," said Lombard anxiously, "careful. If you stumbled here——"

"Be quiet," said Hambledon. "I think there's someone coming up."

"What? Can you hear——"

"I feel it. Hurry! You couldn't hide a rabbit here, and we can't get off the path."

As things turned out it was not until they had reached the wider, flatter stretch near the main track to the summit that they heard, down the track below them, the sound of boots on stone and a scatter of pebbles. Lombard ran away from the path and threw himself down behind a heap of fallen branches; Hambledon, who took less concealing; also vanished into the landscape. The footsteps came up the track, turned off it, and strode along the path which led to the waterfall.

When it was quite certain that the man was not coming back, first Hambledon and then Lombard rose to their feet.

"I know that man," said Lombard, "he is the one I recognized at the frontier post. He fired at us."

"He looked a little grim, I thought," said Tommy mildly. "Perhaps he is bringing the news about their dear departed comrade by the wreck of the Porsche. Did you not think so? He had the air of one who hastens to bring evil tidings. Shall we walk on? That mixture of horror and gloating—quite unmistakable."

"I agree. By the way, have you got—what do they call it in your country? First sight?"

"Second sight is what I think you mean. No, but I seem to have a small private guardian cherub who tells me when something nasty is going to happen. Don't you get something of the kind yourself when you're driving? A sixth sense which warns you there's something round the corner and you slow up and there it is, a small boy wobbling on a bicycle or a cow or something?"

"No. Do you really mean that you hear a whisper in your ear?"

"More like someone blowing on the back of my neck. Well, Lombard, there's your gang and there are also my papers. It's nice to know where they are, isn't it? Can you produce a large force of active policemen all armed to the teeth?"

"Certainly. Let us get down to the road as fast as we can. The Austrian Frontier Post will be the best place, but we can call on anyone we meet to help us."

"If only by lending us their boots, my foot-wrappings are not even what they were and heaven knows that wasn't much."

They hurried on past the shelter hut at the head of the hollow called the Hasel Lahne, after which the going was easier. Some distance further down they came upon two men placidly resting upon a sunny bank. They were dressed in good tweed jackets and soft grey *lederhosen*, light woollen stockings, and what Hambledon considered to be quite beautiful stout boots.

"Those gentlemen," he said, "look to me to be exactly the right sort."

"I agree," said Lombard eagerly. "You talk to them, will you?"

"I imagine our dress will take a bit of explaining away, but I'll do my best." They walked on. The two gentlemen glanced up as they drew near but did not appear in the least surprised or even particularly interested in the sight of two men liberally plastered with mud now drying and flaking off in places, simply dressed in one tattered sack each and having their legs and feet tied round with rags.

Hambledon was a little disconcerted. He was ready to deal with curiosity, disgust, or even precipitous flight accompanied by cries of terror, but not this bland indifference. These men merely glanced at him and his companion, looked away again and went on talking; it even occurred to him to wonder for a moment if they were blind.

He walked up to them and began, "Excuse me, gentlemen——"

One of them looked up at him. "Ah, now, this is convenient. Would you be so good as to tell me the time?"

The other was wearing a wrist watch but Tommy naturally

assumed that it had stopped. He glanced up at the sun and said that the time was a little after four.

"After four! Grissemann, we have been here more than an hour."

"An hour? Nonsense, Geisler. Three days."

They both had charming voices and spoke the German of educated men. Hambledon assumed that they were amusing themselves at his expense and really did not blame them considering how very odd he and Lombard looked.

"My wrist watch is a little unreliable," said Grissemann. "It goes very well sometimes and then, again, it will run backwards for an hour or two."

"It has never been the same," said Geisler, "since you boiled it with the eggs last week."

"On the contrary, it benefited greatly by the treatment, except that that was not last week, it was last year."

Hambledon, who was trying to compose an inoffensive request for the loan of their boots, was not really listening, but Lombard edged away and Geisler noticed it.

"Are you anxious to pursue your way? Grissemann, perhaps these gentlemen would permit that we walk down with them."

"Certainly," said Grissemann, getting up all in one movement.

"An excellent suggestion. I was beginning to wonder how much longer we ought to wait. Besides, I want my breakfast. May we, then, accompany you?"

"An honour," said Hambledon. Lombard bowed and they paired off, Lombard with Geisler and Hambledon with Grissemann; they set a pace which the unshod members of the party found it hard to maintain.

"Excuse me," said Grissemann, "what day of the week is it? I think it is Wednesday, am I right?"

"Er, no, it is Saturday," answered Tommy, mildly surprised to find it was still the same day as that on which they had driven away from Seefeld in Walter's Porsche; that seemed a week ago. "Some days seem longer than others, do they not?"

"Not only seem," said his companion, "they are. That is why I have dedicated a lifetime, and the resources of what I have heard described as a not inadequate intellect, to the problem of arresting the precession of the equinoxes. This business of having different sorts of time, as it were, sliding back and forth against each other is no longer to be endured."

Hambledon came to the conclusion that if this were a leg-pull it was going on for a long time. He decided to change the subject.

"You and the Herr Geisler are fond of walking upon the hills?"

"Not particularly. It is the Herr Direktor who urged it upon us. We were all together, four of us and the Herr Direktor, for the exercise in the fresh air, you understand, when unfortunately the Herr Direktor slipped and sprained his ankle and had to sit still. He sent one of the others for help and one of the others stayed with him so we others came away by ourselves. By the way," Grissemann dropped his voice, "a word in your ear about Geisler. He is a charming fellow and a brilliant historian; he was about to be appointed Professor of Mediaeval History at Heidelberg University when he had his accident. So they did not appoint him, after all. A pity, I sometimes think. After all, when we were boys we always thought all professors were a bit —you know—" he tapped his forehead—"did we not? I should not think, even now, that anyone would notice much difference if one of them really was, would you? But quite harmless, I assure you. What's the time?"

The situation being now sufficiently clear to Hambledon, he was not surprised to overhear Herr Geisler explaining to Lombard that it would not be wise to attach much importance to anything the Herr Grissemann said. "Unfortunate fellow! A brilliant mathematician once, quite brilliant. Sad, is it not? But quite harmless, I assure you. You hold your females in high esteem, do you not? Even admitting them to your tribal councils?"

"I—I—of course we do. Naturally," said Lombard, and glanced over his shoulder at Hambledon.

"This is the greatest moment of my life," said Geisler triumphantly, "when I meet face to face, in the flesh, a living representative of our primitive forebears. We seem to have gone back in time. I will ask Grissemann presently. What tribe are you?"

"I may not tell that name," said Lombard, who was beginning to enter into the spirit of the thing. "It is not to be spoken. Hush!"

"I understand. But tell me—there is so much I want to ask that

I do not know where to begin—is it true that you take your wives everywhere with you, even into battle?"

"Men do. I am not married, myself."

"Then who made that robe you are wearing? Look, Grissemann. This is the very cloth woven by the hands of these chaste but unpolished women who followed their menfolk into battle—may I have it?"

"Battle? No. I war not with white-skinned children," said Lombard magnificently.

"No, no. Your robe, may I have it? Oh, give it to me; it is more precious to me than all the jewelled vestments of the Vatican itself." Geisler took hold of Lombard's sack. "So firm, so even, if a little worn. Give it me." He pulled at it and Lombard strenuously resisted.

"No, no! I will not part with it," he cried. "Great Chief, my mother wove it."

"Forgive me," said Geisler instantly. "I am greedy and discourteous." He released his hold.

"I will send you another," said Lombard.

Grissemann touched Hambledon's arm. "I think my poor friend is getting rather excited," he said in a low tone. "Let us change the subject. If the clock strikes three too many and it is four hours slow, what time is it?"

"Tomorrow," said Hambledon. Even as he spoke they came to a gate at the bottom of the path and instantly four men converged upon them.

CHAPTER XVI

Oh What An Afternoon

The four newcomers were dressed alike, not in military or police uniform but in brown overalls with a monogram upon the lapels. They formed up in a circle and one of them said, "Your pardon, gentlemen, a moment. You are of the party of the Herr Professor Bauer?"

"That is so," said Grissemann with a polite bow. "He has, perhaps, sent you to meet us?"

"I trust," said Geisler, "that you have attended to the Herr Professor before troubling yourself with us? He had a fall and hurt his ankle."

"The Herr Professor has been rescued, gentlemen, and has been taken to the house of a doctor in Mittenwald for treatment. He was anxious about you, his four patients, and I am happy to find you all together." The man's eyes rested upon Hambledon and Lombard. "Shall we, then, walk on together? I have brought a conveyance——"

"To take us back to our camp?"

"The camp will have to be closed down after the Professor's accident, as I am sure you will understand."

"To take us home, then?"

"To our Ruheheim for tonight and home tomorrow. It is too far to go tonight," said the man in what Hambledon had already recognized as a professionally soothing voice. "Let us, then, go on together."

"Just a moment," said Lombard. "This gentleman and I," he indicated Hambledon, "are not of the Professor's party, although I must admit that we look a little odd at the moment. I am Lucius Lombard, of the Austrian Special Police, and this is my colleague the Herr Hambledon of British Intelligence. We must get to a telephone instantly. I must contact the Austrian police at Innsbruck."

"Certainly, mein Herr," said the man, "there is a telephone at the house and the quicker we get there the sooner you will speak to your friends." The words were perfectly civil and obliging but the manner was still soothing, and Hambledon's hackles rose.

"I think," he said to Lombard, "that we had better get on by ourselves. We cannot, now, be far from the frontier post."

"I agree," said Lombard. "You," addressing the four men, "are from the Ruheheim Mental Home, are you not?"

"Why, yes, mein Herr, but you need not let that trouble you. We are on the telephone there and that is what you want, is it not?"

"I'm not going to any mental home," said Hambledon. "The matter is extremely urgent and every moment counts. Once that gang in the hills gets away again we are done, Lombard. If these fellows would drive us to the frontier post it will be well, if not——"

Grissemann and Geisler, standing patiently by, caught the note of anger and impatience and reacted promptly.

"If there is going to be any trouble," said Geisler, "I am going away. I want to be quiet. These savage tribes——" He backed away.

"No fighting," said Grissemann, "for the love of heaven, no fighting. I cannot bear it." He turned and ran down the path toward the road and Geisler ran with him.

"After them, Franz," said the man who was evidently in charge of the search party. "Thank heaven they're running the right way." One of his assistants hurried after them. "Now look what you've done, gentlemen! Scared those two harmless loonies out of their wits and like as not we'll have them screaming half the night. From responsible gentlemen like you, is that right, I ask you? You say you want a telephone; I say all right, I'll take you to a telephone; and now that isn't right for you."

Hambledon made to walk away but the worn wrappings round his right foot gave way at last, the puttee-like bandage fell off in loose coils and tripped him.

"There now," said one of the men, materializing just behind him, "you'll have a nasty fall in a minute. Hold on to me," though in point of fact he was holding Hambledon.

"I think we'd better go with them," said Lombard. "As it happens, I know one of the doctors who attends at the Ruheheim; if he's there our troubles are over."

"Oh, very well," said Hambledon, "let's go. How far is it to this car of yours?"

Apparently it was not very far. Hambledon set his teeth and hobbled on.

"Take my arm, mein Herr," said the nearest attendant.

"It would be much more to the point if you lent me your boots."

"Alas, mein Herr," said the man without a smile, "they would not fit."

The path came down behind a cottage from which a rough cart track led down to the road, now plainly in view. A little farther down the track, at a point where there was room enough to draw a car off the way, there stood a small van of the station-wagon type with a door at the back; the door was open and the attendant called Franz was ushering Grissemann and Geisler into it. There was a small competition of the "No, no, after you, my dear fellow" type clearly displayed in gestures, after which they both got in; the attendant shut the door and doubtless drew a sigh of relief.

"Could not the van," said Hambledon, whose feet hurt him, "be driven up as far as the cottage? I see that there are other vehicles there."

"Normally, yes," said the chief attendant, "but we did not like to do so this afternoon. The old man there has died and those vehicles you see are the funeral cortège."

"They are coming out now," said Hambledon's escort. "Had we not better wait here?" They were still a hundred yards or so from the cottage.

"I think so, indeed," said the chief attendant, and glanced rather uneasily at Hambledon and Lombard.

"We can hardly walk past them," agreed Lombard, "dressed like this."

"If you can call it dress," added Hambledon. "It is not even as though we had hats to take off."

"They will not notice us here," said the chief attendant, "behind the house as we are."

"Then I shall sit down," said Tommy, "meaning no disrespect." He sat down upon a patch of turf and Lombard sat beside him while the three attendants talked among themselves.

"Where are they taking him?"

"To Giessenbach. He came from there, all his family live there."

"They've got a long walk."

"That's what they've got the car for, for the old lady."

"She'll miss him. She won't live there alone, surely."

"She's got a married daughter at Giessenbach, I expect she'll go there."

People came out of the cottage and stood about awkwardly. Six men came out together with a burden upon their shoulders and laid it in a farm cart. More anxious walking about and a priest with a small acolyte before him.

"I never realized," said Hambledon to Lombard, "how completely outrageous we look until I saw those people in their decent blacks."

"I know. We should have made quite a sensation at the frontier post, shouldn't we? I wish they'd hurry up, though, time's passing."

One of the attendants glanced at them over his shoulder and spoke in a low tone.

"They talk sensible enough between themselves, don't they?"

"They often do," said the chief attendant darkly; "you can't go by that. Of course it's awkward our not knowing them, but the other two owned up they were Bauer's lot and as for those two, just look at them! I wonder what on earth they have been up to!"

"There's an old song," said another, and laughed. " 'Oh, what a day we're having! Oh, what an afternoon!' "

The procession moved off at last; the attendant by the van at the side of the truck took off his hat and stood with bowed head as the coffin went by.

"Well now," said the chief attendant, "I think we can go. We shall not overtake them and that's all that matters."

The van was lined with wicker and had a narrow bench running along each side. There was a partition behind the driver and the only window was a small barred aperture in the door. Grissemann and Geisler were sitting at the far end opposite to each other and did not even look round when Lombard and Hambledon got in followed by two of the attendants who sat in the middle on either side to keep the patients apart. The door was shut and fastened from the outside and after a moment the van started, bumping and rolling on the rough track and then, after a sharp turn to the left, gathering speed on the smooth main road.

"Do you know this place, Lombard?" Where is it?" asked Hambledon.

"Just short of Mittenwald. No, I've never been inside but I am continually passing it. I hope Ritter's there." Lombard turned to one of the attendants. "Do you happen to know whether the Herr Doktor Ritter is at the Home this afternoon?"

"I could not say, mein Herr. He might well be there and I not see him and in any case I have been out two hours."

Lombard nodded. Hambledon leaned forward to look out at the little square window, but it was too high to show him anything except hill tops and blue sky; he gave it up and sat back in his corner, gathering together all the self-control he possessed. If Lombard's Dr. Ritter were not there to identify him, the situation might well be awkward in the extreme. The evil chance which had entangled them with straying lunatics just when they themselves were looking like something out of Bedlam would be quite bad enough without the fact that time was passing and the gang were free to go where they would and those wretched designs with them. The situation was at once ludicrous and maddening, for the more he and Lombard insisted upon their rank and identity and the spectacular importance of their business, the more likely they were to be given a soothing injection and put to bed in rooms with no handles on the inside of the doors. To lose one's temper, for example, would be quite fatal.

The van slowed, hesitated, turned sharply to the right and began to ascend. Hambledon half rose in his seat and caught a glimpse of the main road going past an entrance with a lodge and iron gates and a lodge keeper at the door of his house. They were ascending a steep drive which turned sharply. He lost sight of the entrance gates and sat down again.

"We are arriving, I suppose?" he said to the attendant next to him.

"That is so, mein Herr. The Herr will be glad of a rest, perhaps?"

"I should be even more glad of something to eat. It has just occurred to me that I am getting hungry."

"That is a complaint that is easily cured," said the man good-naturedly. "It is not to be wondered at, it is the mountain air. The Herr must ask for anything he wants."

The van slowed, stopped, turned round and backed a few yards to stop again; this time the engine was switched off. A moment later the door was opened and they were faced with a couple of wide steps and an open doorway admitting to a long hall with a flight of stairs going up on one hand, various doors to right and left and a further door at the far end which stood open to show a garden with flower beds and shrubs.

Hambledon climbed out carefully and winced when he stepped upon a coconut mat inside the hall. Lombard limped after him. When Grissemann and Geisler got out, Hambledon was holding pathetically by the doorpost but they took no notice of him. They marched side by side and in step straight down the hall and out of the door at the far end.

"Let them go," said the chief attendant. "There's nobody there and they cannot get out."

"Just a moment," said Hambledon's kindly attendant. "I will bring slippers for you and the other Herr. Your feet must be painful."

"Thank you," gasped Hambledon who was, in fact, making the very most of a certain amount of soreness. He thought it unwise to ask for shoes since they might suggest escape, whereas if these good people offered them, that was another matter. The man returned with a couple of pairs of the gaily patterned carpet slippers which the home-loving German so rightly delights to wear by the fireside. Lombard and Hambledon tore their muddy rags and put the slippers on.

"Ah," they said as one man, "that's better," and straightened themselves.

"Let the Herren come in here," said the chief attendant, opening the nearest door. "There are chairs, let the Herren sit."

"Will you please find out whether the Herr Doktor Ritter is here?" said Lombard. "He knows me and can identify me." He walked into the room.

"Certainly, mein Herr," said the man willingly. "At once."

"I suppose," said Hambledon, "you haven't such a thing as a cigarette? I lost mine when my clothes were taken from me."

"I am, myself, a nonsmoker, I am sorry. The Herr Direktor will have some, however, and he will be here in a moment."

"Thank you, I shall look forward to it," said Hambledon. He also walked into the room and the door closed behind him.

"You seem to be settling down," remarked Lombard.

"That is the impression I am trying to give. We don't want to find ourselves hurled into padded cells and given injections to keep us quiet. For heaven's sake, Lombard, whatever happens, don't lose your temper."

"You are quite right," said Lombard gloomily.

"If your friend Ritter is not here and they won't let you telephone, we will make a dash for the van and drive away in it. I don't suppose they took out the ignition key. Cheer up. This is quite a nice little sitting room. They would not have put us in here if they had thought we were bad cases. If your Doctor— here is someone coming now."

When the door opened Hambledon was sprawling in an armchair looking dishevelled but amiable and Lombard was looking out of the window. He turned, but the man who came in was a stranger.

"I am so sorry," he said, "the Herr Doktor Ritter is not here at the moment. He was in this morning and told me that he was going to Innsbruck this afternoon, so I am afraid you will have to make do with me. My name is Schollhorn."

Lombard bowed. "I am Lucius Lombard, of the Austrian Special Police, and this is my colleague the Herr Hambledon of British Intelligence."

Hambledon stood up and bowed and Schollhorn shook hands with both of them."

"Well now," he said, "I am sure that what you gentlemen feel you most urgently want at the moment is a bath. If you will——"

"I blush to admit," said Hambledon, "that it isn't. What I most want at the moment is a cigarette, if you would be so kind. Oh, thank you very much. So kind. Lombard too, of course, how good of you. While we are enjoying these, my colleague has something to say."

"I am sorry to have to meet you, for the first time, looking like this," began Lombard, "for what sort of impression our appearance must make upon your mind I cannot bear to think. Especially after getting ourselves mixed up with those two charming lunatics. Hambledon and I are working together upon a special mission. I am sorry that for security reasons I cannot go into details, but we have been tracing a gang of men who specialize in robbery on the grand scale and this afternoon we tracked them to their hideout in the hills here. Now if you will kindly let me use your telephone I want to ring up the Austrian Frontier Post at Scharnitz and also police headquarters in Innsbruck and call out enough men to take this gang complete."

The Herr Direktor Schollhorn listened attentively to all this and then said, "Yes, I see. But where did you lose your clothes?"

"That's a long story which I will tell you later," said Lombard. "At the moment, where is your telephone, please?"

"In my office, but it is in use at the moment. What about having your bath first and telephoning afterwards when you are more comfortable? And we will find you some clothes, I really cannot bear to see you in such discomfort. Also, one of my fellows tells me that you are hungry. A nice cup of soup to start with——"

"The telephone, please," said Lombard peremptorily.

"I have told you, it is in use at the moment. Now I'm sure you do not want to make trouble, do you? The Herr Direktor Bauer always——"

"We are not the Herr Bauer's patients. I told you who we are. The matter is vitally urgent and I must warn you that if you——"

"Please do not try to intimidate me, Herr Lombard, please. I am sure you do not wish me to call my fellows in and give you an injection. No, no, let us at all costs be quiet and reasonable. A bath and a nice supper and a good night's rest—I am sure that what with your gangs and losing your clothes and spending all those hours in the open air you must be tired to death. Come, then, let us go. I expect your rooms are ready by now and the water is always hot——"

"The telephone——" began Lombard in a furious tone, but Hambledon stubbed out his cigarette end, got up and took him by the arm.

"Come, Lombard, we are being discourteous in face of the Herr Direktor's kindness. I must confess my bones ache for a nice hot bath and I am so hungry I could eat the soap! Lead on, Herr Schollhorn, we follow."

"Oh, very well," grumbled Lombard, taking the hint. "We are in rather a mess, are we not?"

"There, now," said Schollhorn in a satisfied tone, "I was sure that you would be reasonable." He got up and held open the door for them to pass.

"Lead the way, Herr Direktor," said Hambledon, and put an arm as far round Lombard's waist as it would reach. "Hold up, Lombard, you are going to sleep on your feet."

Lombard's eyelids drooped and he sagged against his friend. The Direktor smiled and walked into the hall. Instantly his visitors exploded into action, leaping out of the front door, down the steps and along either side of the van.

"Push her when I take the brake off—now! That's it, come on!"

The van rolled away, gathering speed down the gradient as Hambledon switched on, put the car into gear, and started the engine. Behind them rose the voice of the Direktor.

"Stop! You can't get out, the gates are shut. Franz! Karl! Heinz!"

"I wonder if it's true that the gates are shut," said Lombard, coyly tucking his sack round his thighs.

"They are," said Tommy Hambledon, rocketing round the last bend. "Hold tight!"

The gates were of wrought iron, tall, spiked, and unclimbable but not unusually sturdy. The lodge keeper came running out when he heard the van and leapt back for his life as it shot past within a yard of him and hit the gates squarely in the middle. There was a resounding crash as one leaf fell down flat and the other swung drunkenly open on one hinge; the van's windscreen fell out in pieces; one front wing came up in a demented Nazi salute and the other crumpled against the bonnet; the radiator disintegrated and water spouted out upon the road.

Tommy wrenched at the wheel and managed to turn the van towards Scharnitz though it took him the whole width of the road to do it. A police motorcyclist on patrol coming towards them braked violently and took to the grass verge as they passed in a series of swooping curves.

"Must you swerve like that," asked Lombard, "or is it just *joie de vivre?*"

"I must," said Hambledon, "something's happened to the steering. We'll get as far as we can." He put his foot down but ominous noises began to arise from the engine and a yet louder and more imperious sound followed them from behind. Lombard leaned out and looked back.

"It is that motorcycle patrol hooting," he said. "He wants us to stop."

"You relieve my mind," said Hambledon. "I was beginning to think we were towing the Herr Direktor. Lombard, listen. This vehicle is drawing to its close. I will pull in to the side and stop. He will come up alongside and stop also, sitting astride his machine with his feet on the ground, they always do. The moment the van stops, Lombard, you hop out and run round the back of the van. I shall open my door and literally fall on him. He and his bus will go over in the road. You grab his gun and pull him out of the way and I will pick up the machine and jump on. You will jump on behind and away we go. Is there anything else coming? No? Good. Now for it. Have we got any brakes left? Dear me, yes."

The van drew in to the side of the road and stopped, with its front wheels inclining together; the awful dissonance of noises ceased as Hambledon switched off the engine. Lombard was already out. The police motorcycle drew up alongside with its engine still running; the rider straddled his feet to maintain his balance, pushed his gogles up on his forehead, looked up and began to speak.

"Who are you and what the ten thousand devils do you mean by——"

The door above him opened suddenly and Hambledon, with a

wild peal of maniacal laughter, dropped on the man's shoulders. He and his machine went over in the road; before he could begin to extricate himself he was dragged clear by a second mud-coloured demon clad only in a torn sack and pulled away while the first demon picked up the motorcycle before the engine had stopped and swung himself on it. The second demon, who was so large that the could not possibly be real, then left the patrol lying in the road, ran to the motorcycle and got onto the pillion seat which he overflowed in all dimensions. The horrid vision then went off down the road, travelling fast.

The patrol picked himself up feeling for his gun as he did so, but it was no longer in its holster. He looked about him, but it was not in the road.

"Two of old Schollhorn's loonies got loose and now they're armed. Two armed lunatics——"

"They ought to keep them chained up."

CHAPTER XVII

The Turf Cutter

"Nice machine, this," said Hambledon, bouncing gently on the padded seat. "If it wasn't for those frontier posts we could make a straight run right through to Innsbruck. Comfortable, isn't she?"

"No," said Lombard. "I feel like a sirloin of beef on an ash tray."

"Oh. How sad. Where are we going?"

"Up that track again to the cottage the funeral came from. They were on the telephone, did you notice? With any luck, the house will be empty; it it isn't——"

"You have only to put your head in at the window and say 'Boo!' and whoever is there will rush madly upstairs and barricade themselves in the top attic. Is that the turning ahead of us?"

"Yes. There's a car coming. What will they think?"

"Nothing," said Hambledon, "if we crouch down; we are going much too fast to present details . . . There, I told you so. They barely glanced at us."

"'Barely' is right," said Lombard, tugging modestly at the bottom edge of his sack. "My garment will blow up. Up here, Hambledon."

They bounced and skidded up the rough track to the small level space upon which the cottage stood.

"Round to the back. We want this machine out of sight and probably there's a shed—there is. Let me open the door of it for you," said Lombard, thankfully slipping off his perch. They pushed the motorcycle into the shed, threw some armfuls of hay over it, and hurried out, shutting the door behind them.

"Now for the telephone. If there is no one in the house, the door will be locked—it is. This window will do," said Lombard, picking up a large stone. "I break this pane and undo the catch, so!"

"Yes," said Tommy, as the window slid up, "but does that help you? Silly small windows these cottages have. I'll get in and unlock the door for you." He climbed in, crawled over a table just inside, and dropped to the floor, Lombard walked round to the door and heard, from within, a high-pitched yell and a curse from Hambledon. The next moment the door opened.

"What in heaven's name was that?"

"Quite all right. Trod on the cat. Come on, telephone in here. Look, Lombard, I'm getting uneasy about that patrol we unseated. He won't have any trouble getting help——"

"You get off up the hill," said Lombard; "no sense in both of us being collared. Here's the policeman's gun, you take it. You'll see what happens if he does get help. He picked up the telephone while Hambledon ran out of the house and up the path. It was, as he remembered, open to full view from the road for the greater part of two hundred yards behind the cottage and Hambledon sprinted up it. Carpet slippers are not ideal for running but they are a very great deal better than bare feet. As soon as the rise of the ground screened him from the road he lay down to watch.

A car came along from the direction of the Ruheheim. It had its sunshine roof open and a man was standing up in it, head and shoulders above the roof of the car, looking eagerly about him. He wore the uniform of the German police. They paused at the turning to the cottage and Hambledon held his breath. If Lombard was meeting delay in getting his connection——

However, the car drove on and he sighed with relief, but it was not far to the frontier post—the German one, of course. When the patrol got there and found they had not passed, he would come back, naturally, and others with him.

More cars passed, all going south towards the frontier; their seemed to be a lull in traffic coming north. Of course, the patrol would be stopping any cars they met and saying: "*Entschuldigen Sie mir, mein Herr,* but have you met two lunatics dressed in mud flourishing a large revolver and riding upon a police motor-cycle?" Then, it was to be hoped, there would be interested cries, a shower of questions, and very natural enquiries as to whether it would be safe to drive on. "Armed lunatics? My dear!" Well, it would all help to pass a little time. Oh, hurry up, Lombard!

Lombard came out, put his head round the corner of the cottage to see if the coast was clear, and came bounding up the steep path with the astonishing agility which surprised Hambledon afresh every time he saw it. He got up and went on to the gate which admitted to the forest path; as he reached it Lombard overtook him and they hurried on together.

"It is all in train," he said. "Old Pfeffer, the Chief of Police at Innsbruck—you met him—is at Scharnitz and I spoke to him there, that is why I was so long. He is coming up himself with enough men for the job. They will come direct from Scharnitz, through the woods, to save formalities at the frontier. If I had had longer I would have informed also the German police at Mittenwald, but something seemed to tell me that I had better not linger. Your little cherub, perhaps, is extending his protection to me for the time being." ,

"They will be some time," said Hambledon. "If you can bear the thought, we should get back and keep an eye on that cave or whatever it is of theirs beyond the waterfall."

"I am glad that it was you who first suggested that because, whether you accompanied me or not, I should have had to go there. I am, after all," said Lombard diffidently, "an officer of the Austrian Special Police."

Hambledon looked at him; at the touseled mud-encrusted hair, the earth-stained face, hands and arms, the disreputable and quite inadequate sack, the enormous legs coated with dry mud where they were not streaked with blood from minor scratches, the ineffably domestic carpet slippers, and began to laugh. He laughed until the tears ran down his face; he leaned against a tree and finally sat down helplessly upon the ground.

"You are, of course, perfectly right," said Lombard cheerfully. "On the other hand, you do not look much like a distinguished high official of British Intelligence who doubtless attends his office every day in pin-stripe trousers, a black coat, a top hat and an umbrella."

"Oh, I don't," said Hambledon weakly, and wiped his eyes upon the edge of his sack. "There's one thing," he added, getting to his feet and striding on as though he had never stopped. "I shall at least be washed and dressed again before I meet my staff, whereas you—er—have my sympathy."

Lombard checked momentarily in his stride.

They went on in silence, meeting no one, and turned off as before into the almost indiscernible trail to the waterfall. Some halfway along it Hambledon, who was leading, checked suddenly and Lombard came up to him.

"A stone rolled down," whispered Hambledon, "ahead of us."

"I heard it, too."

"Better get off the track, if we can."

They climbed up the hillside, helping each other, to crouch behind the boles of trees, and waited, but no one came along the trail and they heard no more.

"Stones do roll of their own accord," said Lombard.

"Doubtless. In any case, sitting perched here won't get us anywhere."

They resumed their journey with renewed precautions, but it was not until they were within a stone's throw of the waterfall that they saw the other walker, a small neat figure in a tweed jacket, grey *lederhosen*, and a brown felt hat. Hambledon and Lombard froze in their tracks, but Medeski was going on ahead of them, not coming their way. He was not much concerned, it seemed, with anyone behind him, for he scarcely glanced back but was plainly very apprehensive about what he might meet. His careful reconnaissance at bends in the path made Hambledon's and Lombard's methods appear carefree in the extreme; at the point where it was necessary to clamber down the side of the river bed he hesitated for so long that Tommy became impatient.

"I'll give him a helping boot in a minute," he murmured. "Not one of the gang, obviously. Who the hell is he?"

Lombard shook his head. "I haven't seen his face yet."

"Someone else after the papers? Really——"

"They don't only steal papers, you know. I told you. They are jewel thieves as a rule."

"Of course," said Hambledon. "Besides, there is—he's gone."

The man had slid over the edge and out of sight.

"I wonder," went on Hambledon, "how long it will take him to make up his mind to cross the waterfall. Ought we to have offered him a helping hand, or is it, do you think, Medeski?"

"I would have stopped him altogether, if I had not been afraid he would shout or shoot and give the alarm. As it is, the chances are they'll see him and all be out like wasps. Damn the man."

"If he doesn't move a little faster they will all be peacefully asleep, for it will be midnight."

"We have had no news of Medeski," said Lombard, "although we have been looking out for him. I have passed on the description you gave me, for what that's worth."

"Nothing, at the moment, since he's out of sight. How long——"

Lombard touched his arm and pointed. Between the trees it was possible to see, as it were, limited vertical strips of the farther side of the stream. Across one of these strips the same man could be seen traversing, painfully slowly, the rock wall below the terrace.

"If he slips," said Lombard, "he'll go down with the water——"

"And we may never know who he is," said Tommy callously. "Come on. Though I should like to know why he did not go straight up the bank as we did before."

"Perhaps there is a sentry sitting on the top."

But no one hindered them as they crossed behind the waterfall and clambered up the other side. Medeski, by this time, was out of sight round a jutting rock and there was little fear of their being heard for the noise of the torrent. Since he had gone to the left they bore to the right until they reached the face of the great cliff itself, towering above them with a marked overhang. Here was a tree, tilted from its place by some earlier spate to lean drunkenly against the cliff; there was room behind its lifted root for both Hambledon and Lombard to lie hid if they huddled together. Once out of the bed of the stream it was noticeable how soon the roar of the torrent was deadened, for falling water has no resonance; a man may be half deafened one moment and hear only a murmur if he walks ten paces round a screen of rock. It seemed very quiet there on the terrace, so quiet that when Lombard broke a dead twig it seemed as though all the world must hear.

Presently Medeski's head, without his hat, appeared over the edge of the terrace and immediately vanished again. There were steps below as a man came out from the cave entrance and walked away from them, to the right, with a pail clanking in his hand. They dared not lift their heads lest he should look round, and the next moment another man came out, hastily, after the first.

"Karl!"

"Ja?"

"You are not to make that filthy noise. That clanking sound can be heard for miles, you fool! And bring another bucket of coke."

Karl did not answer but the noises ceased, to be followed by the sound of shovelling. The man who had spoken could be heard walking slowly up and down; the smell of a cigarette drifted up to Hambledon's nose. Presently the shovelling ceased and the other set of footsteps returned. The bucket was set down and somebody asked for a light; there followed a low-toned conversation of which the only audible word was *"Lottchen."*

Presently a voice called out from the cave. "Come in, both of you, and shut the door. We want to light the lamps."

The pail clanked once as it was picked up; two sets of footsteps crunched grittily and there followed the unmistakable sound of a door shutting.

Hambledon set his mouth against Lombard's ear.

"I know why that fellow worked round to the front. He wanted to know if the door was shut or open."

Lombard nodded and answered, "They will shut the door, always, before they light up; it could be seen right across the valley——" he stopped abruptly.

The small man in the tweed jacket came quickly and silently from the edge of the terrace; he had taken his shoes off and was walking in his socks. Since he was not facing their hideout but crossing in front of it, Hambledon and Lombard peered at him as he went. He had what looked like a piece of iron bar, about a foot long, in his hand. He turned into the cave entrance, out of their sight, and there was silence for a space.

"Medeski, I think," murmured Lombard.

"I agree. What's he doing?"

Presently Medeski came past them again, walking rather tenderly upon the rough ground. He disappeared over the edge but was back again the next moment with a pair of shoes in his hand. He sat down on the ground and put them on.

"How I sympathize," breathed Hambledon.

"I also envy," muttered Lombard.

Medeski rose to his feet and walked across to a place on the edge of the terrace just in front of the cave entrance. Here there was a patch of wiry mountain turf; he stood looking down at it while he took from his pocket something which he opened, and there gleamed in his hand the blade of a knife. Norz, in the prison infirmary at Innsbruck, would have recognized that knife. Medeski went down on his knees and began hacking at the turf.

"He must have fastened up that door," whispered Lombard, "with that piece of bar he was carrying. He is in full view of it and is completely unconcerned."

"That's right. I expect there's an outside hasp and staple to secure the door when they're away, just in case. But what is he playing at? Little man, what now?"

Medeski had laid down his knife and was tearing at the turf with his hands. It came up easily, being shallow-rooted upon rock, and he stood up with it in his hands, a ragged piece a foot or more across, while his eyes travelled up the cliff face beyond the entrance to a point Hambledon could not see. On second thoughts, the Russian put the turf down, took off his coat and put it on the ground, picked up his sod once more and walked steadily forward out of their sight. Even the sound of his footsteps ceased.

"He is beyond the entrance," said Lombard. "What can he want beyond it?"

Hambledon shook his head; after a minute or so they heard a scraping sound.

"This I cannot bear," said Tommy. "Stay there, Lombard."

He wriggled from behind the roots which had hidden them, thereby collecting more damp mud to repair his camouflage, and slipped away in the shadow of the cliff. Lombard watched him go and was surprised to see how unnoticeable he was against a broken background; unless he moved it was difficult to discern him at all. He was behind a low-hanging branch of pine, looking up, and presently came quickly back.

"There's a chimney comes out up there, Lombard. I say, a chimney, it's a pipe. It sticks up about a foot and that fellow is plugging it with turf. I've got it now. They've got a coke fire going inside, coke makes no smoke——"

"The coke," said Lombard, "of course, the coke."

"And when the outlet is plugged——"

"They die, of course?"

"How long would that take?"

"I have had no experience. Not at once, I am sure of that. They go to sleep, I think, and do not wake. An hour? What do you think?

Hambledon shook his head. "Charming little fellow, isn't he? What a bright idea. But, Lombard, they will smell it——"

Medeski reappeared, walking casually as a man does who has time to waste. He stopped, looking towards the door, and went into the entrance; the next moment he came out again and resumed his turf-cutting. Long narrow strips this time, which were carried into the entrance and disposed of there.

"Plugging up round the door," said Hambledon.

Medeski made three journeys with his strips of turf and finally came out into full view, rubbing the mud off his fingers and wiping them on the grass. He slipped into his coat again, felt through the pockets and produced cigarettes and matches; very leisurely he selected one and lit it, dropped the match and put his foot on it, all with his gaze set dreamily across the valley at the lovely hills beyond, the very picture of a suburban householder who has finished a nice job of digging in the garden and is having just one cigarette before tea. He looked down at the ground beneath his feet, apparently decided that it was damp, and went to sit contentedly upon the same lump of rock which, when Hambledon and Lombard had first seen it hours before, had been occupied by a placid gangster peeling potatoes.

"You know," whispered Hambledon angrily, "I don't like this at all. Damn it, if it were rats being exterminated I shouldn't like it."

Lombard shrugged his shoulders.

"We can shoot him," he said. "We've got a gun."

"We can, yes. But——"

"Exactly. But if we merely tackle him he'll shoot us."

"How long will your fellows be getting up here?"

Lombard shrugged again. "There is this, the gang will be much easier to handle if they are well doped."

"That is quite true. We'll wait, then, for your fellows. I don't think coke poisoning is at all sudden; it has to get into the blood stream if I remember correctly."

More time passed. Medeski drew a small paper parcel from his pocket and unwrapped it to display a roll which he ate with every sign of enjoyment.

"If I'd known he had that," said Hambledon ominously, "I would have dealt with him long ago. My insides are rolling round and round looking for something to absorb."

"There was probably some food in that cottage," said Lombard sadly. "if only there had been time to look."

They sighed heavily. Medeski finished his roll, screwed up the paper, threw it over the edge, and wiped his fingers on his handkerchief. After that he lit another cigarette and practiced blowing smoke rings.

A little later Medeski turned his head sharply as though he heard a noise from the cave door; the next moment Hambledon and Lombard heard it too. A confused scraping sound as though someone were scrabbling at the door, followed by dull irregular thumps. Medeski rose to his feet and stood facing the cave.

"They have realized," said Lombard, "that all is not well and that the door is fast."

"I wonder they don't fire through the door; it would at least provide them with some air holes."

Hambledon had hardly finished speaking before there were several shots fired in the cave, five or six.

"That will make the air fouler than——" began Lombard, but Hambledon seized his arm.

Medeski, struck in the body by a half-spent bullet through the door, was staggering with his hands upon his stomach and his eyes closed. He went backwards until one foot went over the edge and the other slipped; he fell, clawing frantically at the wet soil to save himself. But he was upon the spot where he had previously cut the sod and he was clutching the outer edge of the rootless turf. It tore away under his weight and with one thin, continuing scream he fell from sight. The scream ceased abruptly and there was silence.

CHAPTER XVIII

A Nice Old Man

"You know," said Hambledon, sliding out of his resting place, "that was really rather sad."

"Why?" said Lombard the realist. "I know he did not initiate all this trouble, but he was not a very nice little man."

"It wasn't Medeski I was grieving over; it was the fact that he's taken his cigarettes with him. However. Well now, about these men in here?"

They walked across to look at the door. It could be fastened from the ouside by a staple and padlock, but the place of the usual hasp was taken by a short length of chain. Medeski had pulled the chain up tight and pushed the last possible link over the staple. The short iron bar had been used as a pin and about a foot of surplus chain hung down from it. Hambledon pointed at it.

"If we let that chain out a few links," he whispered, "they would get enough air to remain alive till your party come."

Someone inside fell against the door and slid down it.

"I do not like it," whispered Lombard. "Let us take out this packing, perhaps there is enough of a gap under the door to serve them."

They dragged out Medeski's narrow strips and threw them away; there was a barely perceptible gap below the door, less than half an inch but presumably it admitted light for immediately there came a voice from within.

"You out there! Please open this door. I will pay you well."

"Do not shoot any more," said Hambledon. "If you were to kill me you would never get out."

"No, no, we will not shoot——" the voice broke off in a spasm of coughing.

"Very well. Those papers you stole at Basle. Slip them out under the door and I will let you have enough air to breathe."

"Who the devil are you?"

"Never mind. Push out the papers," said Hambledon, flattening himself against the side of the entrance and motioning Lombard to do the same.

"Go to hell!"

"Certainly," said Tommy amiably, "but I think that you will get there first." He skipped nimbly outside the recess of the cave entrance as a couple of exasperated shots crashed through the door. "That was Eugene speaking," he added as Lombard ran across to join him.

"They are not, it seems, yet *in extremis*," said the Austrian mildly, but Hambledon held up his finger.

It was immediately plain that there were divided counsels raging inside the cave. One hoarse voice said: "Give him anything. Anything! Only let me breathe."

"Fool, he will but take them and walk away."

"But it is a chance—a chance——"

"Let us live! You must let us live!"

"Those bullet holes," said Hambledon, "are not big enough to do them any good with no draught drawing in."

Lombard shrugged his shoulders. "For me, they will be just as well dead as alive. You, I observe, are a philanthropist."

More arguments in the cave.

"Give them up—give them up——"

"I cannot bear it, I——"

"Please, please——"

There followed a hollow crash as though a form went over.

"Erich is gone. Eugene, must we all die?" Snuffling noises along the bottom of the door and feeble thumps as of hands beating upon it.

"Oh, very well. It will do no good but if you insist, the blame is yours, remember that." Eugene's voice was weak and dragging; when he tried to shout through the door it failed him in a fit of coughing and he rapped sharply with his knuckles instead.

"Well?" said Hambledon. "You are just in time, I was going away."

"I give the papers—you open the door?"

"Enough to let you breathe."

"No good—open wide."

"It's all you will get," said Hambledon sharply. "Those papers, quick."

He and Lombard closed up upon either side of the door and heard scrambling noises inside.

"They are all on the floor," murmured Tommy. "Air better by the floor."

"Then you can let out the chain without too much risk," said Lombard, "since you have set your heart on it. Not too much or that Paulus will slip his hand out and undo it."

"Three or four links will do."

The scrambling sounds returned to the door.

"Be careful," whispered Lombard. "He may fire when he knows where you are."

Hambledon slipped out of the recess and returned with a thin switch of pine dropped from some armful of kindling. By that time the corner of an envelope was emerging from beneath the door, in jerks, slowly.

"He is holding the other end," said Lombard under his breath.

"Push it right out, you triple-damned obstinate hog," roared Hambledon, losing patience. "Am I to wait your pleasure all day or am I am to put a bullet into you?"

The envelope came out with a rush as far as was reasonably possible; Hambledon swept it clear with his improvised besom, picked it up, and retired outside to see if the enclosure was complete and Lombard followed him.

"All right," said Hambledon with a long sigh of relief. "Now all I want is a pocket to put it in. Under this stone will do for the moment. Lombard, I am going to pull out that bar, let the chain out four links, and ram the bar in again. Will you cover me with our gun and at the slightest sign of trouble let them have it?"

"With very great pleasure," said Lombard formally.

"You know, I've got a sort of feeling that you really mean that. Ready? Good. Though I don't suppose for a moment that there'll be any trouble now, they are not so silly as all that. They want air, not me."

He moved silently to the door, managed to pull out the bar without making any noise, let the chain out four links, and rammed the bar into the staple again. The men inside heard that and threw themselves at the door as Hambledon sprang back.

The door opened barely three inches, no more; Hambledon and Lombard, peering round the outer sides of the recess, saw faces appearing one above another in the tall narrow opening. Not, of course, entire faces but vertical sections thereof, mainly noses and open mouths, and the gasping noises they made were clearly audible.

"The bulging nose at the bottom," said Lombard, in the comfortable voice of a lecturer upon his favourite subject, "is that of a person called Karl. His surname is so variable that I sometimes wonder whether he has any legal right to one more than another, so we always refer to him as Karl Fat-Nose. His speciality is strong-arm dealings with watchmen, menservants, and suchlike who try to impede his passage; several of them died. One would have been enough, Karl.

"The thin pointed nose next above is Paulus Caron."

"The one like a white rat only he hasn't got pink eyes," said Hambledon. "I did hear that the Lucerne police wanted him for, if I remember correctly, armed robbery."

"Ah, yes, you are right. I had his name on a list, but as he is also on a list I compiled myself, I am not sure that they will get him. Next up, the nose which at some time must have met with an accident since I am sure that if he had been born with it they would not have kept him, is one Anastasiou, alleged to be a Turk though that may or may not be true. He is a really nasty piece of work, Hambledon. He doesn't like women."

"Don't make me sick," said Tommy, "on an empty stomach. Please. It is such hard work."

"As you wish. The top one, of course, is our Eugene, alias

Horaz the Nitwit, but I will do him the justice to say that the nickname is unfair."

"I agree. Most unfair."

It will be clear that if only noses and mouths are exhibited at a narrow vertical slit, the eyes are not in operation, but at this point Paulus Caron moved his face enough to be able to see out. Lombard, carried away by his subject, had moved forward into full view and Paulus could see him very plainly. His eyes opened widely, his jaw dropped, he uttered a wail like a lovesick cat and disappeared abruptly from sight.

"We did the wrong thing, Lombard," said Hambledon. "We ought merely to have opened the door and walked in and they would all have fainted away."

"There is something in what you say, though it is their doing that we look like this."

"Not entirely. One must be just."

But Lombard's head had turned sharply and he held his hand up for silence.

"Quite right," said Hambledon. "I heard it too."

"I will go and meet them," said Lombard, moving away. "It will be better if someone shows them the way under the waterfall."

"Be careful, then."

"What, of falling?"

"That, too, but I meant you should be careful whom you meet. Remember that your people are not the only men looking for us. There is an angry German policeman looking for his motorcycle and his gun——"

"T'chah! Here, we are in Austria, the frontier line is——"

"And there are those muscular male nurses from Schollhorn's Home of Rest."

That reminder did pull Lombard up; he hung upon his heel, listening.

"With whom," added Hambledon, "we know it is quite useless to reason and it wouldn't do, I feel, to shoot at them. What do you think? If, for example, they proposed letting our prisoners loose?"

"In that case," said Lombard grimly, "I certainly should. In the legs. I will go very carefully and scout.

He disappeared over the bank of the waterfall, from which

direction there came presently cries and countercries and shouts of welcome. Hambledon grinned to himself; he had not believed for a moment that those mental nurses would indeed come so far or tackle armed men in the open, but it was amusing to get a rise out of Lombard sometimes. A good fellow but a little cold-blooded. Well, on his job it was, perhaps, necessary.

Lombard returned, looking a little flushed, followed closely by the smart soldierly figure of Pfeffer, the Chief of Police from Innsbruck, and a force of about a dozen police, all, of course, armed. Pfeffer was also rather red in the face but he had, after all, been walking up a mountain; also he wore an expression of rigid solemnity. At sight of Hambledon his solemn expression, as it were, splintered into a grin and he seized the ends of his grey moustache in both hands and pulled it quite savagely.

Hambledon went forward to greet him and Lombard, in a few brief sentences, made the position clear.

"I do not think that they are in any shape to give trouble," he said, "but they are, of course, armed and desperate."

"We will have them out one at a time," said Pfeffer. "Disarmed, handcuffed, and, as you say, half doped, we should be able to deal with them, I believe. How many are there?"

"Six I have seen," said Lombard; "there may be more." He turned towards the door and the sight of what architects would call his rear elevation was too much for one of the young constables who gave vent to a noise like a soda-water siphon in operation and turned it into a fit of coughing. The man next him kicked him on the ankle; Pfeffer glared him into silence and the operation started.

Pfeffer bellowed his orders through the door.

"You in there! This door will be opened and you will come out one at a time as I call and not before. I will say 'First' and one will come; 'Next' and one more will come, and so on. Singly, one at a time. If more than one come out together, they will immediately be shot down. You will leave your weapons behind. Understand?"

They came out, one by one, staggering, with eyes half-closed and a hand on the rock side of the entrance, breathing in the fresh air in great gulps. One by one they were taken over and dealt with and Lombard counted them off as they came.

"Eugene. Paulus. Erich. Karl. Anastasiou. Marc. Is that all?" The procession ceased.

"Is that all?" repeated Lombard, and moved forward to peer into the cave. Instantly there came a fusillade of shots from within, wild shooting as of one who could not see; the bullets ricocheted from the sides of the entrance, or sang over their heads or struck the ground.

"Who the hell is that?" said Lombard, springing back. "You, Marc, who is that in there?"

"Our leader," gasped Marc, who was being held up by one of his captors. "Our leader—you won't take him alive. He said so. Not alive, he said."

Pfeffer looked at Lombard who said, "Shoot him down, then. None of this scum is worth the lives of your police."

Some of the police were armed with magazine rifles. Pfeffer conferred with one of his inspectors and a man lay down on the ground by the entrance, suddenly pushed his rifle round the corner, and fired the full charge straight into the cave. Before the reverberations had ceased there was a clatter inside as though someone had dropped something, and after that, silence.

They waited, still there was no sound. Hambledon borrowed a hat from one of the police and poked it into view from within. Nothing happened and two of the police, flattening themselves against the sides of the doorway, went in and presently returned, carrying between them the dead body of a man which they laid down on the ground outside.

"No one else there, mein Herr."

Hambledon and Lombard went forward, bent over the body, and uttered loud exclamations of surprise.

"Eisenschmidt! Old Eisenschmidt, from the antique shop!"

Lombard whirled upon the party of prisoners. "Eugene. Who was this man?"

"Our leader," said Eugene. "Been our leader for years. And other men's leader, long ago, and you never rumbled him, did you? Clever, aren't you? Thirty years and more, forty years, I don't know, fifty years maybe he is doing this and you never caught him. Did you?"

"Get away," snarled Lombard, and Eugene was removed.

"Cheer up," said Hambledon, "he fooled me, too. I thought

he was such a nice old man. Never mind, he's dead now." He folded his hands yet more firmly over a packet he was holding to his chest. "Herr Pfeffer, have I your leave before we go to search that cave for something?"

"Certainly, by all means. Do you think there may be treasure in there? You may be right."

"Oh, no," said Hambledon. "At least, yes. Not diamonds, Herr Chief of Police. Our clothes."

He turned to go in; with a yelp of joy Lombard sprang past him and vanished into the decent obscurity of the cave.